THE BLOCKS

AN ETHAN WARES SKATEBOARD SERIES
BOOK 1

MARK MAPSTONE

1

THE GIRAFFE

Ethan Wares got himself in direct line with one of the marble blocks outside the Network 27 TV station building and ollied into a frontside 50-50. The wax from yesterday was still good and the grind glided effortlessly. The ten AM sun hadn't yet risen over the building, but within an hour the warmth would pull out the smokers, slackers, and phone-callers. Turning at the end of the path, Ethan caught his reflection in the blue-tinted UV protected glass and looked for any employees behind it. He held a stare whilst carving back around, but only saw himself looking back. Someone would have been there, coffee in hand, watching him whilst at the photocopier or trying to focus on their email. He flipped his middle finger up at the window, pushed off back towards the block, and ollied into a backside 50-50. He landed slightly heel-side, held the grind, and felt three large black blocks send a satisfying click through his feet as he rode over the joins. As the end approached, he leant slightly on his front truck, lifted the back and twisted into a crook-grind before hopping off.

No-one cheered, clapped or acknowledged the make, just the clickity-clack sound of his 54mm wheels on the herringbone tiles. Security would have spotted him on CCTV by now and it was only a matter of time before they arrived. He took another run at the blocks and manual-rolled the first then ollied up into a nose-slide on the next, sliding as far as he could before hopping off the end.

Still no Security.

Before he arrived this morning, a couple of younger skaters warned him that Security were alert as they had been asked to leave within five minutes.

'You might get ten minutes in if you're lucky,' one of the local grommets, Mike, said. 'It's a new guard, too.'

Ethan shook it off. 'I get special treatment.'

Mike's friend dug around in his bag and pulled out a sharpie. 'Could you sign my board, please?'

Mike sniggered.

'What?'

Ethan scribbled his name and handed the board back. 'That okay?'

'Thanks,' the boy said. 'Where are you going this week?'

Ethan didn't know, he never knew, that was the deal.

'All I know is it's going to be hell.'

'That's nuts. Do they…?' The kid rephrased his question. 'Is it all planned out?'

Ethan chuckled. 'No, I swear it isn't.'

'See I told you,' Mike said. 'He thinks it's all set up.'

'After the last one,' the boy said, 'when you fell from that building…'

Ethan pulled up his hoodie to reveal the scars on his waist. 'These aren't special effects.' He pinched his skin proving they were real. 'That isn't the worst of them either. I've got stitches in the other arm.'

Mike punched his friend in the shoulder. 'Told you.'

Ethan pulled down his hoodie. He was late and wanted to get a roll in before work.

'No Hermanez?' Ethan checked with Mike.

'Maybe, but we didn't see him.'

Eduardo Hermanez was a short-legged Mexican security guard with a furious temper who made it his mission to ruin every skate the locals attempted at Network 27. The riders slowly learnt that Hermanez made less noise the closer he got. What started as a South American explosion at a distance, quickly diffused to a sparkler once up-close. Skaters ended up mocking him, answering back, but then getting bored and moving on once they'd finished winding him up.

A new security guard meant a new type of trouble and Ethan saw it as a breath of fresh air to his otherwise dull morning. He put his board down to hit the blocks again, then saw the capped head of a man in uniform at the side of the building.

It wasn't Hermanez.

This new guard was tall, slimmer, and younger than the others. He'd soon pile on the weight once slipping into the CCTV-watching routine for eight hours a day. Security was always on a power-trip, shielded behind their privately funded uniform. *You might as well be wearing a fancy dress*, he thought. He skated towards a block and ollied into a frontside 5-0.

'No skateboarding here,' the guard shouted. He used his radio aerial to point to the exit.

The bridge of the guard's nose was flat like an infant which made his eyes look too far apart, and the brim of his hat pushed out his ears like a Giraffe.

'Ahh get off. I'm not bothering anyone.'

'Leave the property now, please.' The guard put his radio to his mouth. 'I'm with the individual now and will be escorting him off the premises, over.'

'Jeez,' Ethan said. 'Give a guy a break. What harm am I doing?'

'Leave the property now or I'll make you leave.'

A few staff members had gathered at the first-floor window.

'Oh, will you now?' Ethan said. 'How are you going to do that?'

The guards demeanour changed, as he realised he needed a different script from the advanced chapter of the Security Guard's Handbook.

Ethan grinned, flipped his hood down, and revealed his bald head. 'Go back to your playhouse and make tea for your boyfriends.'

Hermanez and another guard came out from around the side of the building.

'I've got it covered,' the Giraffe shouted.

'Like hell you have,' Ethan quipped. 'It looks like you've shat yourself with worry.'

'Don't let him intimidate you, Dennis,' Hermanez said. 'This one's a regular, always causing trouble.'

'Dennis,' Ethan said. 'As in penis?'

The Giraffe was sweating. It was clearly his first day on the job and he didn't bank on having such a challenge straight out of training. He put his hand on a small leather pouch attached to his belt and pointed his radio in the direction Ethan needed to walk. 'If I don't see you leaving in the next ten seconds, I'm obliged to use force to remove you.

This is private property. We have signs up.' The guard then turned back to Hermanez. 'It's ok, I've got this.'

'He really doesn't. I think you'll need to take over.' Ethan sucked up a ball of phlegm and spat it at the guard's shoes, narrowly missing.

'Five seconds,' the Giraffe said.

'Stuff your five seconds and your make-up bag.'

'Leave now!' Dennis took a wider stance which made him look thinner than ever. One knock to the knees would drop him to the floor faster than a playing card pyramid.

Hermanez stood just behind the Giraffe. 'What a piece of shit. Don't let him get away, Dennis.'

Dennis grasped a small device on his hip and took a dry gulp which yanked his Adam's Apple up an inch.

'You know your problem? Insecurity.'

'Leave!' the Giraffe stepped hesitantly forward.

Hermanez reminded Dennis the five seconds were up.

'Ok, ok,' the guard said, 'I've got this.'

'C'mon, on then.' Ethan stepped forward with his arms wide. 'Get it. Get it!'

2

THE PLANET

The Giraffe pulled his hand away from his hip and lunged a cracking blue spark from a taser straight into Ethan's stomach. He froze, with fists clenched as every muscle tightened with a violent shake, his eyes were pinned wide open, the veins on his neck pulsed like worms and it felt as if his blood was trying to boil him from within. Just at the point where Ethan felt as though he was going to pass out, the guard released the device and he fell to the ground groaning in pain, dribbling spit on the floor and slowly moving back into consciousness. Hermanez and the other guard began laughing hard. The Giraffe looked back at them, shocked and perplexed by their callous response. The Giraffe quickly remembered his training and knelt down to check Ethan's eyes for pupil dilation, ears for blood, and then his hands and pockets for weapons.

'You fuckers,' Ethan muttered through desperate gasps for air.

Hermanez was bent over in hysterics and rubbing his eyes with his fingers. The Giraffe pulled a small plastic case attached to a lanyard from Ethan's back pocket and he immediately realised his mistake. He'd checked so many IDs all morning. Every member of staff at Network 27 flashed the same card at him for the entire hour of entry duty. Occasionally, Dennis was obliged to select an employee at random and take a closer look, checking Name, Picture, Date of activation, and scanning the card for notice of expiration. Ethan's card clearly showed his details, including the same bald head, wide eyes, large lunatic grin and missing tooth. The Giraffe realised that he'd been set up and felt Hermanez' hand on his shoulder.

Still laughing, Hermanez said, 'C'mon, you've got to see the funny side.'

'Oh my god,' the Giraffe said.

Ethan managed to sit up but didn't make any attempt to get off the ground.

'How was it?' Hermanez said to Ethan. 'Just as good?'

Ethan wiped the sweat from his forehead and some saliva from his mouth with his sleeve. 'It hurt as much as the last time.'

'I'm really sorry.' The Giraffe held out his hand to help Ethan up. 'I had no idea who you are.'

'I didn't think you'd do it,' Ethan said to him taking his ID card back.

Hermanez agreed, 'Think of this as your training complete, Dennis.'

'I can't believe you did that to me.'

'I think I wet myself a bit.' Ethan checked the groin of his trousers. 'Yeah, I have. This'll bring another dynamic to my meeting with Flint.'

As Ethan and the guards walked slowly back towards the entrance of the building, the doors opened and Ethan's brother, Heston, made his way out on his crutches.

'You're late,' Heston said. 'You should have been here twenty minutes ago. Yet despite that, you seem to have announced your arrival really well.' Heston pointed up at the floor above them full of people at the windows.

'I thought it would be rude to be early,' Ethan said. 'Besides, who wouldn't want to remember their first day on the job?'

'How's the treatment going? Have they given you a new course yet?'

'Nope.' Heston shook his head and pulled a pot of pills out of his pocket. 'These things are playing havoc with my sleep as well.'

'Hey, you look after those. Do you know how much they go for on the streets?'

Heston gave a little smile. 'Look, I know you don't want to be here, and I appreciate everything you're doing to help me out.'

Ethan tried to smile back but could only glance away again and punch the lift button a few more times. When the lift opened, Ethan held the doors from closing and let Heston inside.

'Have you heard from the Insurance company?'

'Nothing solid yet.'

Ethan couldn't believe the process would take so long to rectify. 'How bad does a car accident need to be before they stump up the cash?'

'It's not that,' Heston said. 'They know you were driving and…'

'How? Who told them? Because I didn't.'

'I don't know maybe they've got you on camera somewhere. You know how these things go.'

'They're still going to pay out though? Right?'

'I'm sure they will, but until then. Thanks.'

'See you at the top.' Ethan let the doors close on Heston with him on the outside.

'Race you up,' Heston said just before the doors shut.

Heston waited in the lobby of the tenth floor, fully aware that Ethan would be taking his time to climb the flights to the top. There was a time when Heston would walk with him, but not now. Injuries aside, they often came to blows when Heston would try and join him on the stairs for support. Ethan would tell him to go away and leave him to it. He knew his anxiety was his problem and swore to deal with it his own way. In truth, he couldn't bear to have others around when he was so under pressure, when he felt so vulnerable, and when he was on the cusp of crying. Therapy was helping, but not fast enough; his therapist told him it was as much about coping as over-coming.

'You may never be cured,' she'd say, 'but you can learn to live with what you have.'

Ethan found his own way of coping: telling everyone to fuck off and leave him alone.

Once he reached the top floor he wasn't even embarrassed to fall through the double doors into the corridor.

'You seem to be a little out of breath there, E?'

'I just wanted a closer look at your shoes. Very nice,' he said on all fours. 'Seriously, this is all part of the daily fitness regime for an all-star athlete like me.'

'You used to look in better shape.' Heston pointed at one of the Network's many pictures on the wall. It was of Ethan five years earlier, and several stones lighter, jumping down a double set of steps outside the Police building. In the background were two officers chasing after him.

'That was a great day.' Ethan pressed his palm into the stitch on his side.

'For you maybe. However, you probably don't recall the hours of paperwork, apologies and court fines we paid to get you and the photographer released.' Heston knew that Ethan was stoned at the time and now only had these pictures as a vague reminder. Ethan took a moment to catch his breath and looked at a few more framed photos, 'How many of these things have they got in here?'

Heston began walking down the hall towards the Accounts department, 'How many pictures?'

'No, I mean, how many of me?'

'Jesus. Give it a rest, will you?'

N27's 10th floor was home to very few people, namely: Finance, Management, and meetings. The meeting rooms were big, a big waste of space. They were always places of complete yin and yang: you either got hired in one of them or fired in one of them. Someone's boss would be sat at one end of a table with an employee at the other, nodding obediently, whilst the chalk fingers of their accomplishments scraped down their career blackboard leading to a pay rise of sod-all. It looked too much like school to Ethan.

'Pricks,' he said.

'Maybe,' Heston said, 'but they pay our salaries.'

'If one of them didn't turn up tomorrow. Would the place screech to a halt?'

'Play your cards right here and you could have one of those offices one-day.'

'The only reason I'd want one of those offices is to jump from it.'

Every month Ethan visited the 10th floor he'd only recognise a handful of people. Many faces would be brand new, as if they'd just walked out of University via the suit shop and straight into the elevator. He'd try and catch their eye for a hello, but headphones would go on, calls would need to be made, and conversations would be cut short as a deadline would surprise them.

Ethan knocked his skateboard into every desk as he passed.

'Do you have to do that?' Heston said.

Ethan waved across the room at one of the women carrying a stack of files to a shelf. 'Do what?' he said.

She looked away again quickly.

'Oh, that,' Ethan seemed to snap out of a daze and acknowledge his skateboard as if it had manifested out of thin air. 'Yes,' he said. 'Yes, I'm afraid I do.'

3

STATS DON'T LIE

Finance was also on the top floor, where payments were either paid or delayed, including the one in Ethan's pocket that should have been paid in full and sitting in his bank account. For some reason only half of it had arrived and Bennett was the man who could sort it out. Bennett was short and fat, and carefully nurtured an extra chin with facial hair to compensate for his rapidly receding hairline. Ethan always held back from mocking the man's expanding waist, as his own seemed to be catching up faster than he wanted. Bennett reminded him of those middle-aged men who sometimes attempted to ride a skateboard to show they still 'had it' when they clearly didn't. 'Are you alright mate?' Ethan would say looking down at a man in a heap in the bottom of a bowl with his forearm broken like an extra elbow. 'I think I broke my arm,' he'd say. *Fucking idiot,* Ethan would think.

'You seen Bennett?' Ethan said. 'I want to give him a big hug and tell him I love him.'

'A big hug?'

'Around his throat.' Ethan searched all the faces at their desks as they walked through the aisle.

'Probably not the fastest way to get a cheque paid.'

The brothers made their way to the Planet office, which resembled a glass ball jammed into the side of the building. It was as if the Gods of Architecture had spat a marble into a concrete cube of cheap entertainment. From inside, the ball allowed visitors to walk out over the edge of the building allowing guests to react in one of two ways: feeling sick or taking photographs. On Ethan's first visit he signed his five-year contract to film weekly docu-shorts for N27's new independent channel for youth entertainment. Ethan could still remember the morning well: the meeting was just after he'd received a series of phone-calls from his sponsors cancelling his contracts. For the most painful thirty minutes of his skate career, his phone was red-hot, and his soul was crushed. His only hope of saving his finances was N27. Somehow, they hadn't heard of his ability to fuck-up. Instead, they must have had the email from a different decade, one which showed his ability on a board, his athleticism, his clean image and bright white smile. When he first walked in through the door, they were ready to call security and have him ejected.

Ethan let his brother in through the door first and saw the Managing Director of Entertainment, Celina Flint, at the back of the room reading through some paperwork. She was a small soft-spoken woman in a light grey suit and bob of grey hair.

'You're late,' Flint said removing her glasses.

Ethan sat across from her. 'I knew you wouldn't mind waiting,' he said.

Heston sat between them and gave a brief smile at Flint to acknowledge the late start and an apology. Ethan picked up a pencil and began spinning it around his fingers like a drumstick.

'I don't have much time for you today,' Flint said.

I'm surprised you've got any time for me, Ethan thought.

It was unusual for Ethan to meet Flint; each week Heston would hand Ethan the next location and walk through the arrangements, cameras, security, knowledge of the area, the obstacle, and what was possible given the likelihood of being disturbed.

There was a Plan B too. There had to be. Lately the locations had become trickier to film. It was just bad luck, but the frequency was not good. Ethan needed something to go well for once and having Flint in the meeting was not a positive sign. Ethan's relationship with Flint was thinner than the top lace on a kickflip foot.

Flint seemed rattled in some way. Her watch face was caught on her jacket cuff, and it was never caught. She hadn't noticed, but Ethan noticed and that meant she wasn't her usual self.

'So, what have you got for me this week?' Ethan held out his hand and Flint slid the file across the desk to him.

'A fifteen-foot granite ledge in Liverpool,' Heston said. 'No-one knows about it yet, and it's a temporary art installation.'

'What's the catch?' Ethan said looking through the pictures in the file.

'No catch,' Flint said. 'It's been flown four thousand miles from Dubai to Liverpool. The granite is from an illegal mine in Brazil closed after a decade of civil unrest. The fatality rate was so high the local miners were literally fighting to stay alive whilst being paid to work. This piece of stone was believed to be from the last cart pulled to the surface. It has great cultural significance.'

'It looks perfect. But isn't it going to be guarded?'

Flint didn't answer. She just lifted her hands slightly as if puzzled by Ethan's question.

'So why is it in Liverpool, exactly?'

'It's Art,' Heston said. 'When does art ever need a reason to be anything?'

'When were these pictures taken?'

'Yesterday,' Heston pulled out some surveillance shots of a crane lowering the block into position, 'We've got a very small window of time. The ground crew just took the fencing down this morning, and we think you'll have until midday tomorrow, then the media will be all over it.'

'Tomorrow?'

'We need you on the train in an hour,' Flint said. 'The tickets have already been booked, your cameraman has already been notified and will be on the train with you.'

Ethan reached into his back pocket and pulled out a piece of paper. It was his pay slip. He unfolded it and slid it across the desk towards Flint. 'Can you tell me why I have only been part-paid?'

Flint didn't look at the slip. 'Probably just an accounting error. We'll look into it.' Flint packed up her paperwork, 'We need you on the train now.'

Ethan didn't feel like getting up. The cheque was important. His bank account was low, and the bill for Heston's treatment needed to be paid in twenty-four hours. Ethan knew that Flint's suit alone would have cost more than his monthly wage.

'Wares?' Flint said. 'Time to go.'

Ethan looked at Flint and still didn't feel like responding. Eventually he spoke, 'Why are you here? Heston could have done this.'

Flint paused. The question had pinned Flint to the spot; it must have been serious.

'I've just come from an emergency board meeting as there was a review of the current schedule. It's not looking good. The viewing figures are down across the network, and some serious overhauling is needed. Nothing has been decided yet, but the impact is going to be company-wide.'

Ethan dropped his pencil and let it roll off the desk onto the floor. 'I thought you said the figures were good?'

'Oh, they are,' Heston said. 'Really good, but just for your show.'

'That,' interrupted Flint, 'is not the issue.' She gave Heston a glare. 'Ratings are averaged throughout the day and whilst your show might show a small spike there's nothing to indicate that it's down to you.'

'Well, who else could it be down to? The stats don't lie.'

'We're all a team here, Wares, and we all work together to succeed. Viewers are fickle and we all know too well that resting on our laurels…'

'Our what?'

'… is a very dangerous path to tread.'

'So let me get this clear. We know people are turning up to watch me skate some crazy location every week, without fail, and we know, once the show is over, they stop watching. What's the confusion?'

4

NO SKATEBOARDING

Heston pulled out a sheet of paper with the viewing figures on and slid his finger across a row of numbers. 'Last week, for example, saw a 25% increase…'

'Great,' Ethan said, 'So the way I see it is I'm an asset.'

Flint slammed a file onto the table and slid back in her chair, 'No, Wares. You're not an asset. You're a liability. Can I remind you of Blackpool? £9,000 in damages; Peterborough: £4,500; Winchester: £2,500 and a court order, I believe?' Flint turned to Heston for confirmation, who reluctantly nodded.

'… And yet, I'm still here, week after week, being thrown in a hole and having to dig myself out, to keep N27 afloat.'

Flint had had enough. 'Don't think for one second that you'd still be here if I had anything to do with it. You've screwed up so many times I've lost count of the number of bills we've had to pay to keep people happy.'

Normally, Ethan would have settled down once he'd fired Flint up, but today he had the upper hand. 'Maybe you should pick better locations next time? How about sending me somewhere decent? Somewhere with hot and cold running water and nice people?'

'I can't help it if that's where you skateboarders like to go.' Flint made her way around the desk and towards the door.

Ethan closed the file in front of him. 'I'm going to need that cheque paid.'

'We'll get on to it.'

'I can wait.'

'We need you on the train now, Wares.'

Ethan picked up the cheque by its corner, let it hang for a moment, then gave it a little shake.

Ethan got off the bus at the train station, walked up the steps to the platform, and ran his palm along the round blue handrail all the way to the top. The rail had a thin white paint scratch line from a board on it as if drawn casually by a child with a crayon. The line covered two-thirds of the rail, until level with the top step: which was low for a board-slide. *It looks like a make*, Ethan thought. The steps were a ten-set, painted yellow on each edge for visibility which was as useful for skating at night as it was for pedestrians. Seeing a strobe of yellow flashes pass underneath when ollieing always felt satisfying. Jumping steps was slowly fading from his bag of tricks; when boards were free it was meaningless to destroy a few, but now packages had stopped arriving at his door every month, the thought of returning to the skate shop to pay the full retail price was not an enjoyable prospect.

Upon reaching platform 2b, the announcement came through the speakers that the 11:44 train was on time and due in fifteen minutes. Ethan rolled on his board towards a bench and put down his back-pack; the platform was fairly clear. He popped an ollie and heard the echo bounce down the platform before doing another and another; then a backside 180, a fakie kick-flip, and a switch-flip. After a few more flips he started getting into it and did a heel-flip, nollie-flip, and a frontside-flip. The last trick didn't go well; he primo-ed it straight on the arches of his feet and landed backwards taking a hit to his tailbone and elbows. As he laid there on the floor, he noticed a few student types on a bench. A kid with a red cap filmed discreetly on his phone, until he saw Ethan notice him and put it away.

'Hey, did you get that?' Ethan shouted over whilst getting up off the floor.

The kid shook his head as if he had done something wrong. Ethan gave his back a stretch and rubbed his elbows.

'Uh, yeah,' the kid said. 'I think I did.'

'Let's see that slam. I want to see what went wrong.'

The boy cued up the footage and held the screen up, which Ethan reached for and had to pull quite hard on in order to release the boy's grip.

'Not enough flick, that's all.' Ethan handed the phone back. 'Can you film another?'

He didn't wait for the boy to answer and rolled off towards the other platform pillar, then turned and pushed back again. Just as he was about to squat down for another attempt a voice bellowed at him from behind.

'No skateboarding on the platforms, please,' a guard shouted.

Ethan was too committed to stop and popped the board but lost his concentration and kicked it away.

The guard bellowed again, 'No skateboarding.'

Ethan didn't acknowledge the man striding towards him and kept rolling around. The kids on the bench did though and glanced back and forth between them.

When the guard reached Ethan, he was checking his trucks for a loose bolt.

'If you skate again,' the guard said. 'I'll have to

notify the station Police and you'll be removed immediately.'

'Why?'

'Because it's dangerous; and it's the rules: so, if you don't like it, you can leave.'

An excuse Ethan had heard too many times before, 'What danger? The platform is empty, there's no trains or people and I'm in control of the board, so what exactly is dangerous about it?'

'What about him?' the guard pointed towards a man further up the platform with a bright yellow suitcase talking into his phone. 'Look, as I said, I don't make the rules.'

'And yet you're applying them when it isn't necessary. What do you get paid? Minimum?'

'That's none of your business. And no, I don't.' The guard was momentarily distracted.

'Do you want a pay rise?'

The guard chuckled. 'What, you're going to get me one, are you? With your skateboard stunts? Don't make me laugh.' Then he turned to walk away.

'Yeah, I can get you a pay rise.'

The guard paused, 'How?'

'Your boss,' Ethan continued. 'My dad knows him, the old guy, I forget his name.'

'Jones,' the guard said. 'What about him?'

'My dad was drinking with him just a couple of weeks ago, and I picked them up from the pub and drove them home. He was saying about he's planning on retiring early.'

The guard shifted on the spot and stepped a bit closer.

'He said he's got to find a replacement, but no-one is showing any sign of leadership. They're all just doing their job, but that's not enough. He said he needs someone with initiative. I just thought I'd give you the heads up, that's all. You seem like a decent guy.'

'He said that?' said the guard.

'I swear on it.'

'How do I know you're not lying?'

'You don't,' Ethan said. 'But it's your call. I'm just passing on the information. You can either think about it, or I'll tell that guard over there.' Ethan pointed at a short guard further down the platform dragging a bin-liner and a brush.

'No,' the guard said. 'No, let's just keep that between us. Okay? Look, I'll turn a blind eye for now, but we've got cameras everywhere,' he pointed up at the CCTV. 'No skating around people and definitely not when a train arrives. Got it?'

Ethan nodded, 'Sounds good to me.'

The guard looked at his colleague working further down the platform, then at the kids on the bench, and walked off. Ethan got back on his board and rolled around feeling the tightness of his trucks underfoot.

'Hey,' the kid on the bench said. 'Was all that true?'

'No, total bullshit. Can you film this front-flip again?'

Ethan pushed out towards the far pillar and looped back towards the kid with the phone. He hopped his feet into position, crouched, popped, lifted his arms, slid his foot up off the end as the flip rotated around 180 degrees beneath him before landing on his bolts in a tiny plume of diesel dust.

5

WEED

As the train came into the station Ethan picked up his bag and joined the platform queue. The engine passed them, then first class, a food carriage, a couple of standard classes, a quiet class, and the final engine. Despite the quiet platform earlier a surprising number of people gathered and began filling the available seats. A couple of noisy families headed into one of the carriages and many others headed into the other to avoid them. Ethan waited in the queue whilst an old lady battled with her suitcase up the steps and shuffled ever-so-slowly through the carriage past the storage and toilets. When the queue came to a halt, Ethan looked down the line and saw the guy with the bright yellow suitcase still on his phone blocking the aisle. The old lady politely asked him to step aside, and despite touching his arm lightly, still couldn't pull him away from his phone. A few people in the queue became impatient and decided to go and sit in the other carriage allowing Ethan to stand just behind the old woman. Once she tried and failed again to get him to move, Ethan had had enough. He politely asked her to step aside so he could talk to the gentleman as the sixty-second whistle had just been blown from the platform guard.

Ethan tapped the guy on his shoulder, who turned, and looked confused at Ethan's face, just inches from his own.

'This your case?'

'Yes,' the guy said and then he slowly turned back to his phone call.

Ethan picked up the suitcase, stepped back towards the doors, and threw it onto the platform until it skidded to a halt some metres away.

The guy hadn't even noticed until Ethan tapped him on the shoulder and pointed at it, 'You best go and fetch it then,' he said with a smile.

The man's mouth dropped open, and he pulled the phone slowly away from his ear as he realised his case was no longer with him. He saw the guard wave his paddle in the air, and knew he only had seconds to spare to fetch it and get back on the train. He pushed past Ethan and ran out onto the platform, but it was too late, the doors had already started to close. The man protested at the guard on the platform and pointed back at Ethan, who just waved back at him and gave a little smile. The old lady walked to a nearby empty seat just as the carriage began pulling out of the station.

'I can't condone what you did,' she said, 'but the silly sod deserved that.'

Ethan found a free seat and plonked himself down in it. His phone rang: it was Heston.

'Buddy,' Ethan said. 'Yep, I'm on the train now. Is he? What's he look like?' Ethan sat up straight and looked up and down the aisle for the description Heston relayed to him of the cameraman: late twenties, stubble, tall and skinny.

'Should have a yellow camera case with him, you say?' Ethan realised what he had inadvertently done and leant his head against the glass to catch a final glimpse of the yellow case disappearing from view. 'Yeah, OK, I'll look out for him.' Ethan hung up. 'Bollocks,' he said.

'Oh dear,' the old lady a couple of seats back said. 'Trouble?'

'Yeah, you could say that.'

Ethan put his phone away and leant back into his seat. Cameramen were hard to find, and good ones were even harder. With nothing more he could do now, he decided to catch up on some sleep for the rest of the journey.

. . .

Ethan woke to the sound of the boys from the station racing through to the other cart; he grabbed one of them and asked where they were in the journey. The kid yanked his coat back and declared he didn't know.

The old lady from the opposite seat in the aisle leant forward, 'We're just outside Birmingham.'

'Thanks.' Then immediately he began to consider his dilemma. He needed a filmer and fast. If the edit was ever going to make it to N27 in time he needed someone with skills and equipment. The chances were slim. He considered going through his contacts to beg a favour from some old friends. It would be a futile attempt as so many filmers were working for the same companies who had sacked him. Up ahead the boys had gathered in-between the carriages, *Maybe I could get that kid to film?* Ethan thought. Phone footage wouldn't be suitable but there was a chance he knew someone who would have better gear. Ethan got up and shouted down towards them, 'Hey!'

One of the boys saw Ethan with his mouth gaping open, his breath heavy from the broken nose he failed to fix many years ago. Suddenly all the boys turned and looked through the carriage window and then disappeared from view again. Ethan ran down towards the doors. 'Hey,' he shouted again. He hit the door button a few times until it opened and immediately smelled weed. The kid with the red cap made his way down the aisle, looking back occasionally and stumbling as his backpack knocked the seats. Just as Ethan reached the next set of doors they closed on him again. Upon opening the boy was nowhere to be seen.

'Where are you?' Ethan muttered. The toilet door was next to him, but not quite closed; he could see someone moving inside and pushed through it startling the boy.

'Jesus!' he said. 'Take it, take it.' He held a bag of weed up at Ethan's face and cowled against the back wall of the toilet shielding his face.

'Thanks,' Ethan said taking a good look at the impressive buds inside. 'But I don't give a shit about your weed. You think I was after this?'

'What do you want then?'

Ethan turned and looked into the carriage hallway to see if anyone was behind him. He closed the door and locked it.

Almost immediately, Ethan's chest muscles began to tighten and restrict his lungs; constriction continued up into his throat allowing only small and quick breaths. The small open window was pitiful and despite the train's speed, air flow was minimal. The kid was still cowering in the corner as if waiting to be mugged. Ethan tried to find something to focus on and relax, but nothing within this two-metre square plastic box could provide the distance to settle his stomach cramps and sweating palms. Inside the bag of weed was a freshly rolled spliff the length of his index finger.

'Give me your lighter.' Ethan pulled the joint out, stuck it in his mouth, sparked up the end and took a long drag. He held the smoke in his lungs for as long as he could before blowing out a white plume.

'Oh, that's good,' he said and handed the joint over to the kid. 'Go for it,' he said. 'What's your name?'

The boy relaxed and took back his joint. 'Bradley.'

'Gotcha. Shall I call you Brad or Bradley?'

Bradley shrugged nonchalantly and took another long draw. 'Whatever,' he said. 'Why were you chasing us?'

'I wasn't. You ran. Why did you run?' Ethan took another drag on the joint.

Bradley pointed to the bag of weed.

'Oh right, fair enough. No, I need a cameraman and mine is, um, no longer available.'

'Don't tell me: the yellow suitcase guy?'

Ethan tilted his head a little as if he was trying to make up his mind as to the value of a new cameraman. 'So, let's just say that you proved you could frame a shot at the station, and I wondered if…'

'I'm getting off at Birmingham,' Bradley said.

Someone tried the toilet door handle; they pushed and pulled a couple of times and gave up.

'You know anyone in Liverpool who could do it?'

Bradley thought for a moment, 'I do actually. I mean, I don't know them, know them, but a past graduate at the University came into our school in the summer and did a talk on film making.'

'Really?'

'Hey, don't blast it all.' Bradley put his hand out to take back the joint, but Ethan didn't give it up.

'Why?' Ethan nudged the fat bag in Bradley's lap. 'Is this not enough?'

Bradley let it slide.

'So, who is this person? Have you got a number for them?'

'Maybe.' Bradley got out his phone and started to search through his contacts. Ethan got up to try and push open the little window a bit more, it wouldn't, and so he blew his smoke out of it and noticed the Birmingham New Street station sign on the wall.

'Is this your stop?'

Bradley turned and looked out of the window gap. 'Shit,' he said grabbing his bag and running out of the toilet before Ethan could turn around. When he did, Bradley was gone. Ethan still had the joint and thought it would be a shame to waste it, besides it was working a treat on his anxiety.

6

URBAN EX

On arrival at Liverpool station, some two hours later, Ethan awoke from his stoner sleep and found himself at a table seat. He quickly looked for his bag and found it beside him, packed full with spare clothes and essentials for an overnight stay. The queue for the exit moved slowly and Ethan waited for everyone to leave before he stood up. He never saw the point in rushing for the door and having to wait in the process whilst people wrestled with their luggage at either ends of the carriage. As he stepped off the plate onto the platform, he was met by two uniformed Station Police officers.

'Can I ask you your name, sir?' said the approaching officer.

'Ethan. Ethan Wares. Why?'

The officer glanced at his colleague and

nodded, 'Okay, Mr Wares we'd like you to accompany us to the station.'

'Why? What have I done?'

The officer took out a notepad and read from it. 'We have had a complaint that you assaulted some students on the train prior to Birmingham; had an altercation with a passenger at Bristol Temple Meads, and have been smoking Marijuana during the journey; which accounts for two offences: smoking in a confined space and possession of an illegal substance.'

Bradley, Ethan thought, 'This is bullshit. The weed was for medicinal reasons.'

'So, you admit to the offences of smoking and possession?' The officer motioned to the other, who pulled out his handcuffs and grabbed Ethan's wrist.

'Hey,' Ethan pulled his arm out of the officer's grip. 'You can't do that; I haven't done anything wrong.'

'Resisting arrest, Mr Wares? That's another offence.'

The two officers lunged quickly pinning his arms and bundled him to the floor; the handcuffs snapped on with practiced precision. As he was lifted off the floor by his forearms, still protesting his innocence and struggling, some bystanders caught the arrest on their phones.

'Don't worry,' a man said, 'I've got it all on camera.'

'Thanks,' Ethan said, but then he realised the man was talking to the Police officer.

Once Ethan had been processed at the station, he was shown to a cell.

The guard unlocked the door and held it open for Ethan, 'Now be good, Mr Wares. You've got company.'

On the opposite side of the small room sat a young woman in her early twenties wearing water-proofs and covered in mud as if she'd been potholing.

'Hi, Roomy,' he said with a smile. 'Did the fashion police arrest you?'

The woman briefly acknowledged him before returning to focus on the drain in the middle of the floor.

Ethan sat on the bench opposite and waved to try and catch her attention.

'Let me guess,' she said finally. 'You're one of these people who are completely innocent and yet for some reason, despite not being able to see an entire wake of stupidity behind you, today you just did something extra stupid, which landed you in here. And as soon as you get out, you're going straight back to doing it again?'

Ethan was impressed, 'That's a pretty good assessment. Can I try now?'

'Be my guest.' The woman sat upright a little and shuffled back against the wall.

'You're a heavy crack user, who had been terrorising neighbourhoods with a spate of break-ins throughout the night by...' Ethan paused to think, '... by crawling through the, um, sewers? And leaving a calling card saying, you've been sludged.'

'Nice,' she said with a small smile. 'There's a degree of accuracy in there actually, but not sewers; not today, anyway. So, what put you in here?'

'I'm working,' Ethan said. 'I mean, not right now, but I might as well be, as I tend to end up in places like this, occasionally.'

'What sort of work?' she asked.

'I work for a TV station, Network 27. I have a show about skateboarding and I do little skate missions each week for them.'

'Oh, children's TV. Cute. How's that been working out?'

'It's good: free travel, expenses, fame. The standard thing.'

'And yet you're in a police station.'

'Well, it hasn't been quite so good for a little while.' Ethan got up and looked out through the little window in the door to see if the guard was around. 'Hey,' he shouted. 'Shouldn't I be getting my phone call about now?' With no answer from the officers Ethan went back to his seat. 'What about you, then? Go for it. Surprise me.'

'Have you heard of urban ex?'

'Can't say I have, but it sounds good already.'

'It stands for urban exploration photography: people who spend their spare time locating and photographing abandoned buildings and spaces.'

'You do that?'

'No, I document them doing that.'

'Document?'

'I film them. I'm putting together a film about the UX scene, but sometimes it's a little riskier than it should be. This…,' she lifted her finger and spun a circle in the air, '… is one of those occasional inconveniences.'

'Hey, would you film me? I need a cameraman, err, woman.'

'Thanks for the equality vote. I can see where you get your influences. Why would I want to film you? Oh, and I prefer to be called a cinematographer. And no, I won't.'

'Why not?'

'Why should I?'

'I've got to skate a granite block…'

She faked a yawn.

'Hear me out…'

'Go on then, I'm listening.'

'This is a special block. It's been flown over from Dubai and costs a fortune because it's to do with a mine in Brazil or something…'

'Or something?'

'Yeah. Look, I can't recall all the details, but it's all in my paperwork in my bag.'

'So far on the interesting scale, you're up there with a mouldy loaf of bread. Have you got to fly out to Dubai?'

'Jesus, no, you wouldn't get me on a plane for any money. I have a kind of condition.'

'The same condition which gave you the bright idea to smash your tooth out?'

'Probably. This one is more about space.'

'I've got news for you,' she lowered her voice to a whisper. 'Planes don't go into space, yet.'

'I mean, spaces, confined spaces. They freak me out.'

'Whatever. By the way, I'm still not interested.'

'I have to go and skate it in Liverpool. At the Braxton estate.'

Her eyebrows lifted and her mouth opened. 'Braxton?'

'What? You've heard of it?'

'Who hasn't? They don't call it the Bronx for nothing. According to News 24 there were eleven knife related deaths there last year alone. People drive through without stopping in their cars, because they know they'll get jacked. Postal deliveries: suspended. It's a riot there, literally. Whoever's sending you, hates you.'

'Fuck,' Ethan said. He remembered Flint passing him the folder across the table, this was her latest attempt to get him to quit. If it wasn't for the money, he would have done it already.

'Listen, all that bullshit you just gave me: I'm not interested. But to film at the Braxton Estate, now that's interesting.'

'Great.'

'I'm £250 a day - how many days do you need?'

Ethan hoped she didn't want payment today, because the last time he checked his account, the Network still hadn't paid him. 'One day,' he said.

She thought for a moment, 'Then it's £500.'

'Wait, I thought we had a deal at £250?'

'Yeah, you did, didn't you?'

7

AIKIDO

It took another hour until the officer had processed the paperwork needed to release the pair and returned to the cell.

'Ms Dixel Manning. Mr Ethan Wares,' the officer said. 'Come with me to the front desk where you can collect your things.'

Ethan tried to resist saying something witty to the guard on the way out, but couldn't hold back, 'Congrats for wasting everyone's time.'

Dixel followed Ethan out in silence. After Ethan collected his board and bag, he looked briefly inside and saw the tightly wound swirl of clothing colours wrapped around his headphones, phone, wallet and keys to protect them in case he needed to throw his bag over a fence to run from a spot. The officer handed Dixel the paperwork for her third civil offence warning for trespassing in a month which she signed and slid back across the desk. She collected her case from the counter, set everything down on the seats by the wall, popped the lock on the case and opened it. Inside was an expensive RED camera positioned in a little foam hole surrounded by three lenses and battery packs.

Whoa, Ethan thought. He knew little about cameras but recognised quality when he saw it. 'One thing I forgot to mention,' he said. 'I don't suppose you can skate, can you?'

'What?' Dixel stopped putting her possessions away into her pockets, 'Wait, what? Why?'

Ethan knew the answer would be no, but she needed to know that one of the fundamental filming techniques of skating involved a rolling shot. 'Don't worry,' he said. 'I'm not going to need you to do anything crazy…'

'I don't skate.'

'… But you will need a board and be able to roll along with me and film.'

'Film at the same time?'

'Like, duh. It's no biggie, seriously. You just roll and hold the thing.'

'I'm going to need danger-money for this. It wasn't in our original agreement.'

'It's not difficult,' Ethan pushed out through the Police station doors.

. . .

The church bells rang out two chimes, the sun had gone, and the wind had picked up; the city was busy with Saturday shoppers and Taxis. Ethan was hungry and needed to get some food before heading onto the local park. He diverted into a small convenience shop, much to Dixel's surprise.

'You're eating here?'

'Yeah, I'm getting something. What's the problem?'

'This isn't food,' she said looking further down the street. 'Look there's a Noodle Bar just here, they'll have more choice.'

Ethan looked at the sign and ruled it out. A sit-down place with all that fuss: the waiting, the selection, the waiting, the eating, the paying, the tip or no-tip confusion. 'I'm good,' he said. A packet pie was fast and could be thrown in the bag whilst moving. It was stodgy enough to hold back the hunger until later in the day when he could feast properly.

'Jesus,' Dixel said. 'It's literally right here. That place sells nothing but crap.'

Ethan went inside and bought a pasty for £1.49 and when he came out Dixel had gone. After walking past a few shopfronts, he found her sat in the window of the Noodle Bar with a large plate, holding up a king-prawn by her chop sticks and waving it around like a parent trying to get a baby to eat. He sat on a bench and watched her shrug and stuff the prawn in her mouth. As far as he was concerned, she'd just wasted at least four quid on lunch. He took a bite of his pasty and mocked Dixel in the same way she had. She faked a retching motion then shook her head and went back to her phone messages.

The pasty crumbled down his jacket and some pigeons began gathering around him. He flicked the flakes off onto the floor and watched them fight for the pieces. After a while Dixel joined him back outside.

'You missed a treat there,' she said.

'No, I didn't.'

'Too sophisticated?'

'Too healthy.'

The skatepark Ethan planned to visit was south of the river; they needed to follow it for a mile, past the shops and residential estates out towards the main road.

'Tell me something about you.' Ethan said running his hand along the top of the river wall. 'I mean apart from potholing.' They were going to be spending the next 24 hours together, at least, so he thought they might as well get to know each other.

'What do you want to know?'

'You have family, right? Any brothers or sisters?'

After a small, awkward silence, she said, 'I have two brothers: Aiden and James.'

'Go on,' he said.

'Well, Aiden is eighteen months younger than me and is a trainee architect, he's five years into his seven-year course in London. Whilst James is not academic at all; he's good with his hands.'

'How do you mean?' Ethan said. 'Like, he's a labourer?'

Dixel laughed briefly then held up her fists together, 'No, I meant these... He trains in MMA. You know what that is?'

'Sure.' Ethan didn't exactly.

'He specialises in Jiu Jitsu and regularly kicks my ass.'

Oh, that MMA, thought Ethan. 'You're kidding me?'

'Nope. He's training all the time to get ready for the UK championships, and when he's not in the gym, I'm his sparring partner.'

'So, you fight too?'

'Hell no, I spar, I don't fight. There's a difference: zero impact to anything other than the pads.'

'Has he ever done any real damage?'

'To me? No never, other than a glancing blow occasionally, but to others, yes.'

'What's the worst thing you've ever seen him do?'

'Break three guy's legs,' she said.

'Really?'

'No, of course not. He's an athlete not a moron.'

Ethan thought about all the random idiots he'd come up against over the years, and had never considered that any one of them could be trained in a martial art. If they had, his approach of throwing the first punch, hard and fast, and leaving as soon as possible probably wouldn't have been of any use to him.

'Could you show me some moves?'

Before Ethan could prepare himself, Dixel grabbed his hand, yanked his wrist back, lifted his elbow, until his shoulder locked and tilted him back-wards. The pain in Ethan's wrist made his mouth drop open, though no sound came out, and he did everything he could to comply with wherever his body took him. She then pushed her foot into the back of his knee and lowered him to the ground.

Dixel released her hold and helped him back up. 'You okay?'

'Wow, that hurt.' Ethan rubbed his wrist and shoulder. 'If that was Jiu Jitsu, I like it.'

'Not really. It's Aikido,' she said. 'It's a way of using your opponent's energy against them.' She grabbed his wrist again, and demonstrated the same move, but much slower this time and without taking him to the ground. 'Wrist, elbow, shoulder, and knee.'

'Impressive, but I wouldn't go trying that out in public. Attackers don't tend to be as complicit as I was.'

'Really? Thanks. I'll remember that,' Dixel said. 'So, why do you skateboard? I mean shouldn't you have grown out of it by now?'

It's impossible to stop doing something you love, he thought. Whenever Ethan got smacked in the face with that statement, he'd freeze, rabbit in the head-lights style, and stare back weighing up the asker, *is it worth continuing this conversation? Does this person warrant my time? Do I even like you enough to explain anything?* If the answer is no, then he'd just turn and walk away.

'I love it,' he said.

'Like, duh, I figured that out by myself, but *why*?'

He was about to reply when Dixel held up her hand. 'Hold that thought.' She then walked over to a woman on a bench having a cigarette. After a moment of conversation with some pointing, she returned.

'It's this way,' she said.

'Nah.' Ethan pointed in the opposite direction. 'The skatepark is this way.'

'But that's your priority, not mine. I need to get my other case back.'

'What happened to it?'

'It didn't arrive. This one has my camera in, so it never leaves my side, but the other case isn't so important, so it goes by courier; except this time, it didn't get there.'

8

BEATDOWN PARK

At the Depot, a driver pushed a trolly of boxes out through the door as Dixel held the door open. He winked, she smiled. Through the door glass, Ethan could see her in conversation with the man at the counter; she stepped to the side when he spoke and she tilted her head, nodding along and pointing to her paperwork. The man went out the back for a few minutes and returned to check her papers again. It was clear something was wrong. It was missing, but by then Dixel had lost her patience. She leant forward, pressed her knuckles down on the desk, and said something loud and direct. Ethan could see her jawline moving faster than an auctioneer selling a Picasso. Another driver came out and raised his eyebrows.

'You might want to give it five minutes before going in there.'

'I'm happy right here, thanks.'

After a few more minutes, Dixel came out stuffing the paperwork into her pocket. 'They probably have it in there, but they claim the driver didn't have it on his load. Such bullshit.'

'So, what now?'

'Nothing. I've got to wait. We were going somewhere, right?'

'Yeah, of course.' Ethan looked up and got his bearings by scanning the building tops. 'I think the park is this way. Hopefully we can get you a board and see how you roll.'

'And… Why do I need to skate, again?'

'Because it's a winning formula and I wouldn't want to jinx it.'

'Right,' Dixel said. 'So, no room for creativity here, then? Just stick to the formula.'

'No, I can be creative. The Network and viewers want that, but you, not so much. You just need to get me in shot and press the button.'

'It's reassuring to know that you just need a monkey to hold the camera and film your greatness.'

'Thanks, by the way. I appreciate it.'

The dual carriageway rose up out of the city carrying thousands of cars an hour in and out of the shopper's paradise of retail parks, racing, braking, and thumping over the joins in the road like a heartbeat. The view presented drivers and passengers a glimpse into the back gardens of homes filling any available space behind the shops. The further and higher the vehicles travelled out of the city, the fewer the number of buildings, the larger the spaces between them, until eventually the industrial units dominated the horizon.

Hardly anyone knew that Bateman skatepark sat underneath the flyover. Its massive concrete roof echoed around the park with every failed trick, a constant clatter of wood and aluminium against tarmac, timber, and steel obstacles. No-one other than the locals could ignore the huge supporting pillars which met the ceiling and arced into perfect transitions, looping from one to the next. Each section of the arches was cast and dropped into place, one slightly higher than the other to create ledges forty feet long, like a set of giant steps which went on for miles.

'This is it?' Dixel rattled the flimsy wire fence and watched a Mexican wave of supports swing back and forth in their loose fittings. 'I can see why the locals named it Beatdown park.' The entrance gate stood on its own—the rest of the fencing torn away years ago—with an old turnstile allowing one person in at a time like something out of a prison. It was a reminder of measures put in place to control hundreds of young people from various boroughs being squeezed together for the first time. The authorities expected a clash of territorial violence and destruction, much to the bewilderment of the skaters, but it never came, and the park was heralded a community success.

'It's not like anything I remember,' Ethan said. Back in the day, he would have arrived in an old transit tour van and be met with kids banging on the vehicle sides wanting autographs and free products. The queue for the gate would have spanned right around the park, everyone hoping to get in, and the guests would feel like Gods being ushered in for their exclusive and privileged access.

Today the park was a shell of what it used to be. The community support and funding had disappeared, and the combination of wooden and old steel ramps now belonged to the locals. Whatever was valuable got repaired, and whatever wasn't was destroyed and rebuilt. There were a couple of big ramps at both ends of the park, with the middle ground full of smaller obstacles: a driveway with a decent hubba-set down both sides looked like the most recent addition; a couple of flat bars, two little fly-off ramps, grind boxes and a big hip to one side. Outside of the park boundary, huge concrete flat banks connected to the road which ran the entire length of the fly-over, and now, with the fence removed, it was available to skate. The locals had added their own concrete mix to the small curb at the bottom to smooth out the ride, but when hit at full speed, it could still splatter them into the bank. On the other side of the park was a strip of free-standing curbs and dirt used for parking. The bus stop was about twenty metres away and a single phone box kept riders in communication for anyone without a mobile. Despite the dire condition of the park, it had a pretty healthy scene. A number of regular park rats could be found every day blasting around, as well as groups sat on the edges socialising, watching, eating and nursing injuries.

'What's the plan?' Dixel said. 'I need a board, right? Are we buying one?'

'Let's get you practicing first.' Ethan needed to borrow someone's board. 'If you can't get to grips with rolling, then we might need a Plan B.' No-one was going to part with a board if they were riding it. He needed someone who was looking the part; a poser, a grommet, a crap rat who had no skill and used the board just for transport.

A beat-up white Honda pulled in and parked up on the dirt. The driver and young passenger both got out; the kid, about thirteen, had a longboard. Ethan watched the driver come round to the kid and grab a fist full of t-shirt and thumped it into the boy's chest. Ethan began walking over.

'Hey, where are you going?' said Dixel.

'Wait for me here.'

The driver was focused on the kid until he noticed they had company.

'What are you looking at?' the driver said in a *why don't you fuck off* way.

The kid hunched his shoulders to absorb some of the jabs into his chest. Eventually, Ethan got within arm's reach of the pair and stood there. Waiting. The driver stepped closer and stood right in his face. 'You got a problem there, big man?'

'Nope. I just want to watch. It looks like something is about to kick off and I want to join in if it does. I've had enough fights to know if I start them, I'll be back in prison, but my solicitor can always get me off if it's self-defence.'

The driver stared at Ethan processing what he'd just learned, which allowed Ethan to focus on the kid.

'What's your name?' Ethan asked.

'Joe.'

'That's a sweet board. Do you skate it much?'

The driver was put out by Ethan ignoring him, 'Hey, I ain't done with you yet.'

'Oh really? I don't see you doing anything about it.'

A passenger with trainers so green they were verging on the point of luminescence got out from the back of the car and sat on the bonnet. If needed, Ethan would have time to punch the driver out and then deal with the passenger at a leisurely pace.

The driver subtly pulled a small blade from his trouser pocket and rotated the barrel a few times in his hand to catch the light.

9

PERSONAL GUIDE

'Piss off and mind your own business,' he said.

'Oh, that's more like it,' Ethan said. 'Okay, this is how I see this playing out: you might swing that thing at me and slice a little skin, in return, and because you're literally threatening my life, I'm going to have to do something pretty drastic to make sure you don't kill me. So, I'm going to help you out here and give you some warning: I'm going to break both your legs at the knees. At least then I know if your legs are broken, you can't run away, and the police can arrest you. I'm also pretty sure that most people in this park will see everything and back me up.' Ethan stood square on to the driver still holding his blade up. 'So, go for it. Take a swing. I'll try and make the breaks as clean as possible, but I can't guarantee it.'

The driver sucked on his teeth, waved his blade

about a couple of times in Ethan's face and then stepped back pointing the knife right at him. The driver suddenly lunged. Ethan turned and watched the knife catch the sleeve of his jacket. Whilst the driver was off balance Ethan squatted and punched the driver hard straight in the groin. As the driver buckled in two, Ethan threw a second punch into the driver's soft and unprotected throat. The third and final punch went straight into the left kidney and the driver fell back, stumbling, with pain and disorientation, gasping for breath on the dirt. His friend was equally as confused; whether to defend his friend or go to his aid. Ethan picked up the small penknife, looked at it, folded the blade into the shaft and put it in his pocket.

The driver slowly got up off the floor helped by his friend who was told to leave him alone. 'Next time,' he said to Ethan and got back in his car. As he began pulling away from the curb he shouted through the window at Joe, 'I'll see you later.'

Ethan squinted at the car until the dust settled before turning to Joe, 'You're not really going to see him later, are you?'

'Yeah, he's, my brother.'

Ethan felt like a he'd just made a huge mistake. 'Sorry about that.' It was a question more than a statement as he wasn't sure how Joe would react.

'It's okay. He's an idiot.'

. . .

'So,' Ethan said to Joe, 'Are you much of a skater?'

'Hell, yeah.' Joe put his board down. 'Better than all these kids, but this ain't my proper board, so it ain't gunna look like it.' Joe spat on the floor like he'd seen someone else do it.

Ethan asked him for a demo and after a roll up and down the park, it was obvious Joe hadn't a clue what he was doing.

'So why the long-board?' Ethan spat too, then shrugged when he saw Dixel cringe at him.

'Why not?' Joe stamped on the tail-stub and tried to kick the board into his hand; he managed to grab it on the second attempt. 'My other setup is like yours,' Joe said pointing at Ethan's WKND board, 'but better, probably.'

'You mind if my friend here has a go? I'll let you have a go on mine.' Ethan held out his board in exchange, and Joe made the swap.

Dixel stood on it but almost fell straight off as the deck flexed a lot and the 65mm wheels started to move.

'Do you reckon you can stay on it whilst I push you?' Ethan gave her a little push and she glided away from him with her arms out and looked pretty stable.

'Easy,' she said then almost slammed jumping off when she veered into a ramp.

Ethan demonstrated how to balance on one leg,

both front and back, and to use the opposite leg to push and brake. 'Now you try.'

Dixel got back on, left foot first and gave a little push with the right. Luckily her back foot found the board as she placed it and she regained her stability again.

'That's it,' Ethan said. 'You're looking good now.'

Whilst Ethan was preoccupied with Dixel's practice, Joe was down the other end of the park, showing Ethan's board off to some of the other kids. Eventually he skated back.

'It feels flimsy. I bet it would snap on a seven-set. Can I drop off the back of the platform?'

Joe was only a lightweight, but even so, there was no-way Ethan was letting him test out his theory.

'How about I make you a deal,' Ethan said. 'I'll give you twenty pounds for the long-board so my friend here can use it.'

'Is that your girlfriend?'

'No?'

'I think she fancies me.'

Ethan watched Joe watching Dixel bombing about around the bottom end of the park, before realising he'd been distracted. 'So, we've got a deal?'

Joe thought for a bit, 'How about you give me forty and I get to skate this for a while longer?' Joe spat on his palm and held it out for a handshake, 'Deal?'

Ethan declined the shake, but was impressed at the negotiation, 'Ok, forty, but we've got to get going.'

Dixel just caught the end of that conversation, 'We're leaving already? I'm just getting into this.'

'Where are you going?' said Joe.

'The Braxton Estate.'

'Hey, that's where I live,' Joe said. 'I can take you there. I mean, on this, right?'

'A personal guide,' Ethan said. 'That sounds good to me. Dixel, are you okay with practicing on the way?'

'On the streets? I don't think I'm good enough yet.'

'No time like the present to learn.'

Joe picked up his coat from the side of the curb, and Dixel picked up her camera case.

'That looks heavy,' Joe said. 'What is it?'

'A very expensive camera.'

'Want me to carry it for you?' Joe reached for the handles but was blocked by Ethan.

'I'll carry it,' he said. 'So, you can both skate.'

En-route to the Braxton Estate Dixel did her best to get used to the long-board; getting caught out by the drains, and not being able to ride up over curbs frustrated her, but otherwise Ethan was impressed. When the road was smooth and almost flat, she did well. To see her looking relatively relaxed on the board gave him some hope that he'd get the edit completed on time and keep Flint happy.

'What's the surface like there?' Ethan asked Joe. 'Is it bricks, tiles, laid, sprayed, tarmac?'

'Huh?'

'Forget it.'

Joe pushed on ahead of Ethan and caught up with Dixel, then he looked back, 'We're nearly there anyway, you can see for yourself.'

Up ahead several tower blocks poked out from the horizon; cream, blue, and pale green in colour, twenty floors each, Ethan guessed. A grid of nine windows evenly spaced, each punctuated with black satellite dishes like sheet music for Jingle-bells. As the trio rounded another corner, a path led in-between two buildings, opening out again to a larger area with a small play park on one side, parking spaces and some grass around the edges. An open topped bin had been burnt out, the remains of a toaster inside.

'Hey,' Ethan shouted towards Joe, 'Don't ride across the broken glass. It'll get stuck in the wheels.'

Joe looked down and after realising the crunching noise wasn't gravel, he jumped off and picked the board up.

'You want the art-thing, yeah?' Joe said heading down one of the paths. 'It's around this way.'

10

FILM THIS

The three went through a cool, damp underpass covered in graffiti and emerged on the other side where they could see the installation. It was pathetic in scale compared to the arc of flats blocking the blue afternoon sky. A handful of kids were running across the top of the block, chasing each other up and down, whilst a few others were hanging around a kid on a moped. Another girl with a pushchair lit up a cigarette for a friend and blew the smoke in the air as she handed it back. The girls were the first to notice Ethan, Dixel and Joe walking over, then the others looked across and stared before turning back to what they were doing. The kid on the scooter started up his bike and put his helmet on. He yanked back the throttle, leant forward and let the back tyre spin out a plume of blue rubber smoke before releasing the brake and riding off

towards the flats. A kid was tagging up the block
with a chalk pen and another was stabbing his knife
into the surface.

'You know these people?' Ethan asked Joe.

'Yeah, but they aren't friends as such. Just
people.'

Ethan knew there would be an issue trying to
get them to move out of the way, or preferably,
leave entirely. The kid tapping the blade on the
surface was the problem. The block was perfect.
The granite top hung nicely over the edges of the
sides by just an inch and was about three inches
thick. It was clear why a crane was needed to lift it
into place.

'Hey, mate. Don't chip the knife into the block
you'll damage it.'

The kid stopped and looked up at Ethan, then
started tapping again, only harder.

'Mate,' he said again. 'Quit it or you'll wreck it.'

'Fuck you,' the kid said. 'Who are you anyway?
Fuck off.'

The girls sniggered and the boys laughed. The
kid with the blade smiled at his mates.

'Ok, I've asked nicely,' Ethan said giving his bag
and board to Dixel. He then began undoing his
trousers.

'What are you doing, you homo?'

Ethan pulled down his trousers and pants and
squatted on the floor.

'You aren't? Seriously?' said one of the girls. The others began complaining and got up and moved away from Ethan a little.

'Jesus Christ, are you mental?'

'He's got to be retarded.'

'Omg, he's shitting. Someone film this.'

Once Ethan had finished, he pulled up his trousers and put his belt back in.

'What did you do that for?'

Ethan bent down and picked up the shit and walked up to the kids; they quickly moved away. Ethan slapped it down on the block and started smearing it around all over the top and edges.

Dixel retched a little. Joe watched with wide eyes and a smile.

'What the fuck are you doing that for, you prick,' one of the boys said.

'I asked you to stop,' Ethan said meticulously ensuring that no edge of the surface was left untouched. Eventually, once he was done, he stepped back and admired his handiwork and then went to a nearby patch of grass to wipe the excess off.

The kids stood well back from the block in disbelief at what had happened.

'You are a disgusting creature.' Dixel held her sleeve up to her face. 'I thought you needed to ride that?'

'I do, did, but they weren't going to move, so…'

'You literally had no other option? Jesus. So, what now?'

'Well, I know it's supposed to rain tonight, it'll all be washed off by tomorrow. No biggie.'

Ethan walked across to the entrance of one of the buildings and turned on a tap by the wall. He washed and dried his hand as best as he could on the grass and walked back over to Dixel.

'Hey, Joe,' Ethan said. 'I need my board back.'

Joe handed it over and thanked Ethan. 'Can I have a go tomorrow?'

'Sorry, I'll be using it tomorrow,' he said. 'Time to get one yourself. A proper one I mean, not that old longboard.'

'Hmm,' Joe said. 'Reckon they sell some like that at the shop?'

Ethan knew the skate-shop from years ago: it was run by a slimy businessman call Doug Stanford. 'You could try and if he says no, ask one of the skaters for an old board, better still, ask at the skatepark, first. Someone might have an old set up in the garage maybe.'

'Thanks, I'll try that.'

Ethan and Dixel walked out of the tower block courtyard and back to the main road. 'Any news about your camera case?' Ethan asked.

'Nothing yet. They better not have lost it. I'll be hard pushed to replace my stuff.'

'Where are we staying tonight?' Ethan wondered whose floor might be available.

'We?' she said.

'One room?' asked the receptionist at the Travelodge.

'Uh,' Ethan said turning to Dixel.

'Two,' Dixel said. 'What? You think I'm bunking up with you?'

Ethan glanced back at the receptionist, but she didn't react. 'No, I thought you might want to save some cash.'

'I'm not saving anything; this is going on my expenses. I'm working, remember?'

Another forty pounds had just fallen out of Ethan's pocket.

He took the door cards from the receptionist, 'We need to run through the plan for tomorrow so come over to my room in twenty-minutes.' Ethan got a good look at her rear as she walked up the stairs.

'Fine,' she said.

Less than five-minutes after settling into his room Dixel thumped on his door to come in. Ethan cleared his bag off the bed and checked himself in the mirror before opening the door.

'There's no water in my room.' She wheeled her case in and parked it next to the bed. 'I've spoken to Reception; they say it's the boiler on the south side of the building and there's no other rooms available.'

Ethan checked his hot water tap, 'It's all good here.'

'So, I guess you've got a roommate.' Dixel pulled out the sheet from under the mattress. 'Shit. These aren't singles.'

'Hey, don't worry, I can behave myself.'

Dixel went into her bag and pulled out a small pot of pills and put them on the table.

'What are those?'

'Sleeping pills.'

'Are you a light sleeper?'

'They're for you. You're taking two of these tonight; when you're asleep, I'll sleep.'

Ethan noticed a story come up on the TV and leapt for the remote on the bed to un-mute it. The news reporter was covering a piece about the artwork on the Braxton estate and they had filmed Ethan's muck spreading incident from across the courtyard.

'Fuck!' Ethan blurted.

11

SLEEPING PILLS

Dixel got a little closer to the TV and saw the report title across the bottom of the screen, 'Local youths vandalise art installation.'

By the time Ethan got the volume working, a local councillor was being interviewed:

Reporter: Isn't this a case of the locals reacting to Art?

Councillor: We don't believe so; this isn't a case of littering or graffiti, this is a very specific attack, and the whole community is shocked. We've worked so hard to make this project a success and to do this so close to the opening day, is... well, we're all speechless.

Reporter: So, you don't think this is a deliberate slight on the piece as a whole: a £50,000 piece of stone which has travelled over four thousand miles, and it's placed in one of the poorest areas of Liverpool; the local people have every right to be put out by the excess.

Councillor: Whilst we're not denying this piece contrasts with its source…

Reporter: Dubai being the richest city of the United Arab Emirates.

Councillor: … this is not something to dwell upon…

Reporter: The stone was covered in faeces.

Councillor: … and we are working with the Police and social services to identify the youths in question and speak with them.

Reporter: We spoke with a number of the people who say the person wasn't known to them, which leads us to believe he travelled specifically for this purpose.

Councillor: There's nothing to suggest that, however, thanks to the video footage, we have a clear picture of the individual to pass onto the police, and we're certain this won't affect the exhibition's success.

Ethan sat on the edge of the bed with his head in his hands.

'Not the end of the world, surely?' Dixel said unpacking her toiletries.

'Maybe not. But that doesn't mean I'm not going to get one hell of a bollocking when I get back.' He switched off the TV.

'So, this plan for tomorrow: you want to run

through it, or have I got to make small talk with you for the next two hours until you tell me?'

'Uh,' Ethan got up and wandered around to the window. 'It's going to rain tonight, so we'll get up early, get some filming done and get home.'

'And?'

'And what?'

'That's it? That's all you've got? Your grand plan after what we've seen on the TV is to get up early? Jeez.'

'Well, what do you suggest?'

'I'm not suggesting anything, but you might want to plan a little more intensively than that. Maybe someone will be guarding the block tomorrow, maybe they'll put a fence around it, or maybe it won't rain. Did you think about that? Weather reports can be wrong, you know.' Dixel went into the bathroom and placed her bottles on the edge of the bath.

'Well, whatever happens we're not going to know until tomorrow now.'

'Unless,' Dixel shouted through from the Bathroom, 'we go there tonight.'

'I'm not going out tonight.'

'Why not?' Dixel stepped out of the bathroom and saw Ethan screwing the top back on the bottle of sleeping pills.

'You said, two, right? I've just had four.'

Just then there was a knock at the door. It was the duty manager for the evening.

'Ms Manning, sorry to bother you, but we've located another room for you.'

'Excellent.' Dixel took the key fob from the manager. 'Anything to get away from this idiot.'

'What?' Ethan said. 'I've just taken the pills.'

'It looks like you'll be having an early night, then?'

It was one of the best night's sleep Ethan had had for a long time. Those sleeping pills were powerful, but four were too much. He couldn't wake up. He bumped his way around the room to pee, and almost fell asleep again having a shower. Dropping the temperature down to ice-cold barely tightened up his eyelids. By the time he yawned his way down the stairs to the lobby, Dixel was waiting for him.

'You took your time.' She was up on her feet and walking.

'What did you give me last night?'

'Oh, they're good, aren't they? I use them like a taser. If I meet a moron, no offence, I crush a couple of those into a drink, and I know I'm not getting groped in the night.

'You drug people?'

'I look after myself. Sorry, I didn't realise they were going to find me another room.'

'Don't worry about it. Let's just go and get this thing done before things go downhill.'

'Thanks.'

'No, I don't mean you. I mean, filming these things. They never seem to go according to plan, as if the world is out to get me.'

'How so?'

'Take this job. It should be easy. Location, skate, film, deliver. Instead, things screw up every time.'

'You screw up?'

'Not me.'

'You think someone is setting you up?'

'Maybe. Flint probably. She's my boss and has it in for me. The show I work on was supposed to be for her nephew, but there was some kind of paper-work screwup, and I got it. I mean I couldn't believe it myself, but hey, I should count my lucky stars.'

'You don't think you deserved it?'

'I know I didn't. This job was my last chance. What they didn't know, was that every sponsor I had had dropped me that morning. One minute I was hot property, the next I was a leper. People couldn't get rid of me quick enough.'

'Why? What did you do?'

'I don't want to go into it, but, yeah, I was the one who screwed up. So, I deserved it. To get a call from N27, well, I can only assume they hadn't got wind of my reputation.'

'So why didn't they just sack you?'

'They had me sign a five-year deal which they couldn't easily get out of. They've have to pay me the entire value of the my earnings upfront. However, now the ratings are so good, the other directors would crucify Flint if she sacked me without good reason.'

'Lucky you.'

'Yeah, well it should be, if only these locations weren't trying to kill me every week.'

'You could always pick an easier hobby.'

Ethan took in that thought and held a breath that lasted so long Dixel got concerned.

'You ok?'

'Uh, yeah, sure.'

'You've gone quiet on me. Did I say something wrong?'

'No,' Ethan blinked himself back into the real world and saw Dixel was still bewildered, holding up her palms.

'So?'

'So, what?'

'I just said you could always pick an easier hobby…?'

'I can't do that.'

'Can't or won't?'

'It's not that easy. I mean, like, what you're saying is for me to cut off an arm or something.'

'No, I'm not,' Dixel said. 'There must be dozens of adrenaline-fuelled sports you could be doing which gives you the same rush, friendship, challenge. Why stick with this one? What does it owe you? Or what do you owe it?'

Ethan still failed to answer convincingly. He could only um and uh and scrunch up his face, whilst struggling to hold on to any thought long enough to pin a tail on it. Every time he thought he came close to an answer he'd see Dixel's frowning face looking back at him and then he'd lose the point again.

'I've just got to do it,' Ethan eventually said.

He thought it was one of the stupidest questions ever. As if he could give up riding. It would be like asking to shoot your own dog, or give up creating a painting before it was finished, or paddle back across the channel after swimming two thirds. It struck him that Dixel wasn't thinking straight. She needed to compare it to her life, her hobby, her purpose. Would she pack up her camera equipment if no-one wanted to watch her films? Maybe. But he doubted it. *Give up skating, WTF!*

Ethan and Dixel largely walked back in silence to Braxton Estate, there wasn't a real reason, Ethan just didn't have anything to say. Dixel pushed ahead on her board a few times, whilst Ethan carried the camera case, and gave her instructions on stability and foot placement occasionally.

Dixel could push pretty good, get on and off the board smoothly, and her ability to carve around was making him feel she could capture some convincing footage as well. Carrying the camera would be the real challenge.

'Don't watch your feet,' Ethan said. 'Look ahead more and look out for small stones going under your wheels.'

'I can't look everywhere. If I don't look at my feet I'm going to fall off. I'm not made of eyes.'

It was at that moment Ethan realised he didn't know how to explain this basic concept of riding. He knew she had to 'see' everything, yet look no-where specific, or maybe look everywhere specific, at the right time. There was no rule to look near or far, or up or down, but seeing needed to happen all the time, everywhere.

'Ok, just look where you're going, then.' Ethan realised how useless his advice sounded.

And then, as if the world was deliberately trying to prove a point, a stone of minuscule proportions caught under her wheel, skidding the board to a halt, and threw her forward into a brick wall.

'I told you.'

'No, you didn't. You said to look ahead,' she said brushing the brick dust off her palms.

Within another few hundred metres the same thing would happen again. He considered telling her to not put too much weight on the board, but that advice sounded ludicrous as well.

'I'm not very good at this,' she said getting back on the board.

It wasn't true but she wasn't giving up. Dixel didn't appear to be afraid and treated it like a horse that needed taming.

'You surf?'

She didn't.

'You snowboard?'

She didn't either.

'Do you slackline?'

Still, no.

Impressive.

12

ARABIC BLOCK

The Braxton Estate was eerily quiet at 7.30am. The sunlight hadn't completely dried the courtyard from last night's rain, but the block was clean. It was entirely possible that someone from the art exhibition had hosed it down yesterday in preparation for today's media scrum. Ethan couldn't care less about that, as far as he was concerned it was rideable. He threw down his board and the echo bounced around the buildings.

'This is going to wake them up,' he said picking up his board again. 'Perhaps we should limit the riding to a minimum?'

'How long do you think we've got?' Dixel was having trouble lugging the camera case and her longboard together.

'No-idea. I can't help thinking that we're lighting a short fuse.'

The evening had been a warm one and many of the windows above them were pushed open. Skateboarding makes enough noise during the middle of the day, to do it at this early hour was going to create a problem.

This was the first opportunity Ethan had to take a closer look at the block. Fifteen-foot long just as the brief stated, and at just-below-the-knee, it was the perfect height. The granite surface was jet black, with an inscription all around the base. The letters were all distorted and barely legible.

'It's Arabic,' Dixel traced her fingers across the surface of the pattern.

The design wrapped around the vertical surfaces continuously with no spaces in-between. It looked like an intricate tattoo-like decoration; with detail that Ethan had only seen in textbooks about the Middle East.

'Don't you feel bad about riding this? It's so expensive.' Dixel saw Ethan skate off into the distance.

She unclipped the locks on her case and took out the camera.

'Let's get this done, and get out of here,' she said to herself.

Ethan's full loop of the courtyard click-clacked around the buildings. He knew this was the quiet part, once he began ollieing and kicking the board away bailing, people would be up at the windows, immediately.

He popped up onto the block into a fifty-fifty and took the grind to the end. The friction felt good; it slid, but not too much. It also meant he would need to push a little into it. His line began with a frontside nose-grind the entire length, circling back for a nollie-half-cab to switch-crook for as long as possible but he couldn't hold it until the end so he pivoted, flicked a shove-it out and rolled away backwards. The next hit was a combo: a straight backside board-slide, then pushed up into a nose-wheelie and hooked it into an over-crook on the opposite edge. The final trick was a switch one-eighty to 5-0 grind. Ethan held it for as long as he could, but felt the rotation coming and hopped it round backside into a switch-nose-grind. The trick was landed flawlessly, and Ethan looked over at Dixel to see if she'd got it. Instead, she just stood there with the camera in hand by her side.

'Tell me when you want me to start filming.'

Ethan's heart sank.

As if she'd forgotten something, she went back to her bag, digging through the pockets. 'Shit,' she said. 'My light batteries aren't here. They must be in the other case.'

'It's light enough,' Ethan said rolling back towards her. 'It'll be fine.'

'Did you see a newsagent open around here?'

'Yeah,' Ethan recalled. 'Back out on the main road, head towards the junction and there is one on the corner. Can't you film like this?' It was light, but the early morning shadows of the towers prevented the sun from reaching the block.

'I'll be back in a minute,' Dixel walked off towards the gap in the buildings and looked back. 'Keep an eye on the camera for me.'

Ahh shit. 'Hurry up,' he muttered.

Some young kids hung out of the window a few floors up and waved at him. He waved back. Ethan decided to see what else may be rideable in the area. He shut the case and wandered towards the entrance. The heavy doors squeaked open, and the cool damp air inside smelled of burnt newspapers. His board clattered through the doors, but he took care the case wouldn't bash the door frame. Inside, the polished metal lift doors on one side juxtaposed the dark and uninviting staircase: his pulse increased just looking them. Ethan looked back out through the entrance door windows to check if Dixel had returned, and as he did, he sensed that someone had come down the stairs. A sudden hard thump landed on the side of his head, forcing his eyes shut, and left a ringing in his ears. He opened his eyes but couldn't focus. A thud landed into his stomach sent him to the ground in a tight ball of winded pain. The attacker picked up the camera case and walked out through the doors. It took a minute or so for him to get his breath back, sit up and rub away the burning sensation in his ear. He clutched at his stomach, steadied himself on the wall, and felt his ribs for anything broken.

By the time Dixel returned he was laid out on the block.

'Sleeping on the job already?' then, suddenly, 'Where's my camera?'

He tried to sit, but his stomach muscles had already cramped up. A second, slower attempt finally got him upright.

'Where's my camera?'

'I got jumped by someone.'

'Where is it?'

'I'm fine, thanks for asking. And, no, I didn't see them.'

Dixel swore up at the flats and paced around the courtyard talking to herself, regretting her decision to get involved. She roasted him for wandering off, repeating that she was only gone for two minutes. He listened to an almost schizophrenic rant of disconnected thoughts at various volumes, targeting him, the buildings, or herself, everything and no-one, until her thoughts aligned again.

'We've got to get the camera back,' she said.

'I know, I know, the filming,'

'Sod the filming. I don't care about your stupid

skateboarding. I need that camera back, today. Now.'

'We don't know who took it or where it is. There's a hundred homes here. What are you going to do, search them all?'

'If I have to.' Dixel walked towards the nearest building. 'Are you going to help or just sit there?'

'Wait, will you.' Ethan got up and took a few steps. 'We need to think smart about this. The fastest way to get your camera back is not to knock on every single door shouting and screaming at people. You said yourself, this is the Braxton Estate, and people aren't going to welcome you into their homes. They're probably not even going to open the door.'

She stopped and shouted into the air again. She took a few breaths then eventually agreed with him.

'We'll sort this out, don't worry.'

13

MILLER THE TROLL

Ethan's phone buzzed away in his pocket. It was Heston.

'Not good timing, bro.'

'What's going on?'

'Someone jumped me and now we don't have a camera.'

Within a second, the line clicked, and Flint picked up the call. It must have been on speakerphone.

'Wares. No more screw-ups. If that footage isn't delivered by 5pm…'

Ethan held the phone away from his ear and mouthed a silent expletive into the air. Dixel made a hang-up sign with her fingers. Eventually, Flint stopped speaking and Ethan managed to explain that with no camera, there would be no footage, so she needed to relax. Telling her to relax was like telling a wasp to relax. Flint launched into a tirade of contractual obligations and commitment issues for the success of the Network.

'People's jobs are on the line,' she said. 'Not to mention your own.'

'I'm still here, aren't I? And I'm figuring out what to do next. The show doesn't air until tomorrow, so I've got...' Ethan checked the time. 'More than twenty-four hours to get the footage to you.'

'No, the footage needs editing and post-production before airing. We need the footage now. Don't screw up, Wares. Get that footage to us today or you're out and we'll set the legal team on you.'

'She hung up,' he said. It was as if she had no belief in him. He always delivered an edit, and never left a location empty-handed. As far as he was concerned this is just another stupid hiccup and he was getting used to them appearing. The footage would get done today. 'Slings and arrows,' he said.

'What does that mean?' Dixel asked.

'I'll tell you another time. We've got to get that camera back.'

'Thank you. Now you're talking sense.'

Joe rode out on his bike into the courtyard between the two buildings. Ethan shouted and waved at him over.

'Someone whacked me and stole Dixel's camera. Any idea who it could have been?'

Despite giving Joe the best description he could, it became obvious that a white, twenties male wearing grey tracksuit bottoms and a black hoodie could be any number of people.

Joe looked puzzled, 'It sounds like everyone I know.'

'Someone must know around here. How about your brother? Is it worth speaking to him?'

'Probably not. I don't think he likes you.'

'But he might know someone...'

'He's not here today, though. He's had to go to court and won't be back until tonight.'

'Is there anyone else?' Dixel said.

Joe didn't know where to start. 'I know someone who could get you another camera though.'

'We don't need another camera,' Dixel said. 'We need *my* camera.'

'But, c'mon,' Ethan said. 'If we're just stuck here guessing, why not get another temporary camera and get the job done? At least we can all get paid and still be on the lookout.'

'How about this… Stop thinking about yourself for five minutes and care about someone else for a moment?'

He tried to see it from her point of view, but still believed she was acting unreasonably. Knocking on doors would be a waste of time, and the last thing he wanted to do was being forced up twenty floors through the narrow stair-case, and using the lift would be worse. Dixel's irritation made him feel a lot worse. He regretted how he'd lost the most valuable item they had, and he was blaming himself. He felt jinxed.

'When you say someone hit you,' Dixel said, 'what exactly happened?'

'Over there. I was just having a look around and I heard someone, and before I could turn around, bam! It was lights out. I was on the floor.'

'You saw him pick up the camera case?'

Ethan recalled being cheek down on the dirty cold floor with his ear ringing and groaning at the pain of a foot to the stomach. 'Yeah, I saw him reach down and take it.'

'Just one person?' asked Dixel. 'And you're sure there wasn't anyone else?'

'Sure. I saw him leave.'

'How? What did you see?'

He suddenly knew who kicked him, he recognised the same green trainers from the skatepark.

'Who was in the back of the car with your brother at the skatepark, Joe? It was him.'

'That was Carl. Carl Needs.'

'Are you sure?' said Dixel.

'100%. He had those green trainers on. You know where he lives, Joe?'

'Yeah, Flat 882. Top floor.'

Ethan glanced up at the building and muttered *Shit* to himself.

'So, let's go.' Dixel got up and noticed Ethan didn't. 'What?'

'Maybe we could get him to come down here?' He couldn't stop looking at the top floor.

'And maybe we could sit around waiting for Christmas to come, or maybe, just maybe, we could go up and get the camera back. Even if we have to pay for it, I'm sure they don't know how much it's worth.'

'How much is it worth?' Ethan asked.

'About two and a half thousand.'

'Jesus!' Ethan said. 'Let's hope he doesn't know. Is he likely to be alone, Joe?'

'Probably,' Joe said. 'But you said he went out the doors not up the stairs, right?'

'Yeah, that's right. I saw him go through them.'

Joe smiled. 'Then I know exactly where he went. He didn't go home with the camera; he went to Troll's.'

'Who's Troll?'

'Troll is Miller's house on the ground floor. We call him the Troll, because he circles the building in his mobility scooter and goes back inside after a couple of laps. People use his house to collect insurance.'

'Insurance?' said Dixel.

'Yeah, you know, like, so they don't get robbed. You keep the Troll paid and everything is okay. Don't pay, and, well…'

Joe took the pair over to the next building and pointed out the door, then refused to go any further, as he didn't want to get involved. After Joe had pedalled off, Dixel and Ethan hid out behind a bush. With so many windows all around them lining the sky, Ethan knew that they were being watched. The vibe was sketchy to say the least. Joe made it sound like Miller the Troll was running the place, or whoever was working with him. They watched someone arrive and the Troll greeted them at the door, chat for a while, and go back inside together.

'Now we know there are at least two people inside,' Dixel said. She sounded disheartened as if their chances of recovering the camera were quickly disappearing. 'You think Carl is in there too?'

Before he could reply the door opened again and the same visitor stepped out, with something tucked under his jacket. In another few seconds,

Miller whizzed out of the door on his red scooter and followed the path around the flats.

'Let's go,' Dixel said.

'Wait. I'll go in and look around and you keep an eye out for Miller. If he comes back, you'll have to distract him.'

Dixel gave in despite wanting to go and find the camera herself. She couldn't trust him to make sure it was the right case, and took to describing it meticulously, including the scuff marks, the labels from traveling, the colour, size and shape.

'Okay, okay,' he said holding his hands up, 'I've got it, now let me go before Miller returns.'

14

CARL NEEDS

Ethan walked up to the door confidently, as if he had been invited, and after listening briefly he pushed it open. The hinge squeaked and he caught a salt and vinegar scent of chips and cigarettes. The small living room was crammed with furniture, including two sleeping bags on the floor, and a ladies handbag next to one. The ashtrays hadn't been emptied for days.

After passing a filthy bathroom and kitchen, he paused at the back bedroom, where had Joe said they did the business of collections and deliveries. He heard nothing, then gave a gentle push to reveal a room stacked high with boxes and electronic goods; all stolen, Ethan presumed. It was like a stock room in a badly organised charity shop; power cables dangled and tangled around each other; TVs, car stereos, DVD players, kettles, a guitar or three, even a child's electric ride-on toy car. Somewhere inside must be Dixel's camera. He scanned the room for her case and found it in the back corner, behind a computer tower and several laptops. He heaved it out into some space and the case lid fell open. The camera was not inside; its foam space empty. *Shit.* Ethan noticed the light in the room changed from someone entering, and as he turned, Carl punched him in the face. Ethan fell to the floor and shielded himself from further punches and kicks by curling up. He wanted to fight back, but the first blow had left him dizzy. When the punches eased up he kicked out at the side of Carl's knee, which buckled him over, he then grabbed a hand-held hoover and whacked him over the head with it. Ethan sat up and threw another punch, but Carl blocked it with his arm and both tussled on the floor each trying to throw clean punches. Ethan flipped Carl over onto his back and immediately had the weight advantage. He jammed his forearm up under Carl's chin, pinning him to the floor, and punched him in the kidneys and groin. Carl spent more time protecting himself than fighting back. Eventually, once Ethan felt Carl was tiring, he reached up and pulled a stack of equipment over on top of him; the heaviest of which, an old TV, slammed down on his stomach which knocked the wind out of him and left him groaning.

'Where's the camera!' Ethan shouted whilst wrapping a cable around his legs.

Carl spat through a bloodied mouth, 'I've got loads of cameras, take your pick.'

'I don't want any camera, I want *my* camera.' Ethan picked up the case. 'This one; you stole it from me earlier.'

'If you find it, I'll do you a good deal.'

Ethan slid a DVD player off a shelf, which thudded again onto Carl's chest, 'You're in no position to haggle.' Finding the camera in the room by himself was going to be difficult. Ethan didn't really know what he was looking for and was pleased to hear someone come down the hallway.

'You're too late, Dixel. The action's over.'

He opened the door and saw two large men in the hallway: a short stocky thug with no neck and the other taller, with a shaven head, and a face wart which made him look like a potato. They saw Carl tangled up on the floor, realised what had happened and ran towards him. Ethan managed to shut the door briefly but couldn't hold it closed and they pushed through easily. Within seconds, Potato Head had him pinned up against some computer monitors, pressing his forearm against his throat. His feet dangled several inches off the ground and kicked against the big man's shins in a desperate attempt to find a footing. Despite having one-arm free and wanting to press his thumbs into his captors eye socket, Ethan needed all his energy to try and pull his other arm away from his neck and breathe.

No-neck unwrapped Carls legs. 'You alright, Carl?' he said helping him to his feet.

The three of them crowded around Ethan's head watching it turn red and stretch like someone had drawn a face on a balloon.

'Who is this dick?' Potato said getting close enough for Ethan to see the spots on his face.

'No idea,' Carl said. 'Some random who decided to play Judge Judy and Executioner.'

'Want us to take him out for you,' No-neck said.

'Yeah, he ain't no use to me.'

Potato pressed on to Ethan's neck, forcing the last breath out of his windpipe, then slammed a fist into his stomach releasing him into a heap on the floor. Just as Potato set up for a huge kick to the face, Carl stopped him.

'Not here, you idiot,' he shouted. 'Take him outside.'

'Hello?' A female voice came from the front door.

Carl silenced Potato and No-neck with a finger to his lips, and looked around the door. 'May I help you?' he said.

Dixel had already put one-foot into the hallway and had to quickly step back out again. 'I was told you'd be the man to see about a camera? I need something good and as soon as possible. Do you have anything?'

'Yeah, I think I might have something perfect for you. Come in. Please excuse these gentlemen. They're just leaving.'

Potato and No-neck stepped out past Carl and dragged an exhausted Ethan with them. Within a couple of paces, they had dropped him to the floor. The sound of thuds, wheezes, and whimpers of pain came from behind him. As he rolled onto his back he saw Carl on his stomach with his right leg pinned behind the back of his left knee. Dixel had one finger on his foot and just a gentle push made Carl cry out in agony. Potato and No-neck were unconscious on the floor.

'Are you okay?' Dixel said.

'What the hell?' Ethan said, wishing he'd been able to turn around a couple of seconds earlier.

'Did you find the camera?' Then she turned to Carl and pressed on his foot again, 'Tell me where my camera is or I break your knee'

'How did you…?' Ethan said.

'Grab something to tie their legs,' she motioned towards Potato and No-neck. 'They'll be awake soon, and I don't want to have to do this again.'

Ethan grabbed some cables and wrapped their feet, 'You said you weren't a fighter?'

'I trained with my brother a lot; picking up some moves kind of goes with the territory.' Yet again she pressed on Carl's foot, 'Where's my camera? The one you stole earlier from him?' Dixel still had him pinned on the floor in a leg lock. A gentle push got him to talk with agony.

'Back corner; top box,' he said wincing.

Ethan went back into the room and tracked down a cardboard box on the shelf, he heaved it off and lifted out the camera. 'I've got it,' he said.

'And the two battery packs under the foam?'

'Got them.'

A woman in her late fifties stepped into the hallway. 'Is there a TV in there?' she asked. 'Mine was taken just a few weeks ago, I'd love to have it back as I can't afford a new one.'

'Sure,' Dixel said. 'Get in and have a look.' She let the woman pass and got on the phone to the Police.

'Don't call the pigs,' Carl pleaded. 'Just take whatever you want.'

After explaining the situation to the officer Dixel gave the flat number and Carl's name, then hung up. 'They'll be here in a few minutes and asked us to stick around.'

The woman came out of the back room struggling with a big TV, said thank you and passed another person in the hallway coming through. It was a man in his mid-forties.

'Someone stole my son's PlayStation about a month ago. Can I take a look to see if it's there?'

He went on in and dug through some boxes until he came out smiling; console in one hand, controllers in the other. People soon learnt of the stolen items being reclaimed and both Ethan and Dixel weren't interested in stopping them. Despite Carl pleading to let him go, that he'd help them out with anything they needed, and making promises that neither of them thought he had a hope in hell of keeping, Dixel kept him pinned to the floor. The hallway became cramped with people coming and going, so Ethan went outside for space and air.

When the police arrived, Ethan immediately held his hands up and indicated the person they wanted was inside. The officer seemed to know Carl already and was pleased to see him pinned to the floor. Dixel stepped back to let him be handcuffed.

15

MEDIA ATTENTION

'Mr Needs,' the officer said. 'Good to see you again. Hope you're okay down there, you look a little uncomfortable right now.' The officer turned to Dixel, 'What unfortunate reason brought you and this rat together?'

'Theft,' Dixel said. 'Ethan?'

He looked back down the hallway and shrugged his shoulders. 'I'll have some good bruises for you in twenty-four hours.'

'Excellent,' the officer said. 'We'll add ABH to the list.'

'Plus,' Dixel said, 'anything else in here which will help put him away.'

The officer went into the back room and looked around, at what was left of the goods. 'I was under the impression there was more than this.'

'Some residents have already been in,' she said. 'They've reclaimed their stuff.'

'You shouldn't have let them.'

'It's not my job to stop them, either.'

After the officer placed Carl in the car he came back, took both their details, and radioed information back to the station.

Across the courtyard in the carpark, a small group of purple t-shirt wearing team members from the art exhibition gathered around their mini-bus. Some school children queued excitedly alongside their coach as a teacher tried to count them.

Ethan knew that there would be no chance to film anything for the rest of the day. 'Flint's going to string me up. It's rammed over there already.'

'Is there a plan B? Maybe you could skate somewhere else?'

'No chance.' Ethan knew the drill. The marketing department would have been promoting this for days, the directors would have had the location meeting, and the production team would have been gathering complementary footage to wrap around the edit. 'If I don't get this done, I might as well not bother.'

'Maybe we can wait till they have all gone home?'

He still wanted to skate, but also knew that N27 couldn't wait another day for the footage. The window had closed and he felt terrible. It was pointless hanging around. He was sick to death of the place and everyone who lived there.

A crowd had slowly gathered around the block. Dixel didn't think it looked like anything spectacular. She'd seen skateparks before and many of them were huge waves of flowing concrete. This was nothing more than a seat. The carpark across the courtyard, which was usually reserved for residents, was now home to BMWs and Mercedes in wealthy shades of grey and black. The block was certainly attracting a lot of attention.

'I wish they would all go home.' Ethan nursed a cut on his elbow.

'Is it really that amazing? It looks incredibly dull to me. What is so special about it?'

Ethan took out a piece of paper from his back pocket. 'It's a juxtaposition of wealth against deprivation, limited natural materials and the common man.'

'Sounds arty,' Dixel said.

'It's political,' Ethan said.

'Isn't everything?'

'I don't think anyone is reporting on the political angle, though.'

'I'm certain they're not.' Dixel noticed a TV crew on their way over to them. 'Don't look now, but I think you've been spotted.'

A female reporter in a long brown coat was

walking towards them whilst reporting into the camera.

'Oh, jeez. Not her.'

'Janice Mint from Channel One,' the woman said. 'Mr Wares. We're currently live. Please do not swear. Would you be able to comment on accusations that you spread excrement on this valuable art installation? What would you like to say to the owners in Dubai who took great offence, and to the curators of the piece who have worked tirelessly to ensure the event is a success?'

'If you were filming yesterday, you would have seen kids trampling all over it and stabbing it with knives. I got rid of them.'

'Is it true that you've travelled here to skate the piece and inflict your own damage?'

He ignored that one, but she had enough questions and kept pulling the trigger.

'The police will probably realise you're the vandal soon enough and take you in for questioning; do you have anything to say to the residents who believe you've smeared dirt on their local community?'

A man in his fifties interrupted; 'They've just had a scum-bag arrested, so you lot go easy on them.'

Ethan was happy for the defence, however, he noticed the camera crew had drawn more attention and some of the exhibition staff approached with one of the police officers.

'Mr Wares,' the officer said. 'We've been made aware that you're responsible for yesterday's vandalism?'

The exhibition staff looked on smugly and the camera zoomed in for a close-up. Another Police officer stepped up to the first and whispered in his ear. Ethan noticed it was the officer who arrested Carl.

'I'm just going to issue you a caution, Mr Wares,' the first officer said.

The camera spun around to catch the officers face.

'There's no sign of visible damage to the exhibition piece, and because of your involvement in capturing the thief, no further action will be taken. You will be expected to be available for statements. The residents have asked me to thank you and Ms Manning for making them feel a little safer.' The officer smiled at them both, nodded, and began walking back to his patrol car.

Janice Mint pulled on the arm of her cameraman who was recording everything and pulled him over to film Ethan again.

'What can you tell the viewers about the incident?'

Ethan walked over to Dixel examining her camera equipment. 'Is everything okay?'

'No, It isn't.' She held up the camera as if he hadn't seen it before. 'This is my life. Without this, I can't do anything. Watch the camera, I said. You couldn't even do that.'

'You can't blame me for this? I was lumped with a knuckleduster. Look, I'm sorry. It wasn't my fault. You've got your camera back.' Ethan looked up at the camera crew, the exhibition team, the police officers and the bustle around the block. 'How about we get out of here, go and get some food? I'm starving.'

'Leaving is the best idea you've had.'

Janice Mint wasn't letting the pair get away quite so easily and followed them across the carpark. 'Mr Wares, isn't there something you'd like to say?'

'No. I guess you don't have a story. Good luck in your life.'

Getting out of the estate wasn't as easy though. The residents wanted to thank Ethan and Dixel for their part in returning their possessions.

Ethan saw Joe again on his bike, 'Hey, Joe. If this lot clears out give me a call.' They swapped numbers.

'Are you coming back?' Joe asked.

'We're not coming back,' Dixel cut in.

'What do you mean? Of course we're coming back?'

'We? No, you. You can come back if you want. I'm done. I've got better things to do.'

'But I'm paying you, remember?'

'Yes, you are,' she said. 'And I'll be billing you, but I'm still not coming back: my other case has been found and I've got another location I want to check out.'

Ethan's phone rang. It was Flint, again. What could she possibly say that hadn't been said already? Ethan realised that he'd missed his delivery window. The disciplinary she threatened him with would already have been set in motion.

'You going to answer that?' said Dixel, 'Your ring-tone is offending my ears. What is that? White-noise?'

'White-Zombies, actually. You heard of them?'

'Yes, and I don't like it. Make it stop'

Ethan let it ring out. 'It's my boss phoning to tell me my contract is over.'

'Why? Because you didn't complete one little job? Jesus. Screw them. Get another job.'

'Hmm,' Ethan said.

'What? Is that a problem? You look like a capable man.'

'I need this,' Ethan said. 'If you were in my shoes you wouldn't quit either. This is my sponsor.

They pay me and I don't have anything else to fall back on.'

'Wait, will I need tears for this part? As I might have to think about some puppies or something.'

'Not only has my sponsor dropped me, but my friends have as well. Then there's my brother: I'm paying for his medical treatment.'

'Why isn't the hospital doing that?'

'They are, but he needs specialist physio, and it all costs money.' Ethan made a point of looking directly at Dixel. 'I don't want you repeating this to him by the way.' The chances of her meeting Heston were slim, but he didn't want her butting into his business.

'So,' Dixel said, 'you're stuck in a crap job because of your brother's bills and can't leave? I get it. What's the matter with your brother?'

'I crippled him.'

16

A SLIGHT GRADIENT

'Whoa.' Dixel waited for Ethan to continue and when he didn't she nudged him along. 'You're going to have to keep talking because I've got a zillion questions ready if you don't.'

Ethan considered where to start as he had so much to say, but he didn't feel like saying any of it.

'Heston and I used to skate together; he was good at it too. We started at the same time and, being brothers, we were always up for skating. A few years ago, we were being eyed up for a deal with a new company who could only put one of us on the team. We both knew this and decided to compete with each other for the spot.'

'Sibling rivalry, right there.'

'Yeah, but it was mutual and fun too. So, the short story is, we were in a car accident and Heston took the brunt of it. I didn't have a scratch.'

'So, where's all this guilt coming from? Was it your fault?'

'And with Heston in hospital, I took the spot on the team. Some say I shouldn't have, but he would have done the same. I would've wanted him to, at least.'

'Don't tell me, Heston wasn't happy with that?'

'Not by a long way. We didn't speak for ages. He said brothers should stick together. I felt bad but, shit, these things don't come along often, right?'

'Skip to the end…'

'We're hoping the insurance pay-out will cover the physio costs, but until then half my salary is going on it. It's the least I can do. I try and sell some free products I get for extra cash, but no-one wants a board with N27 written across the bottom.' A big WKND sticker covered the N27 logo on the bottom of his board. 'N27 has zero credibility in the skate scene.'

'From what you told me, you're not part of any skate scene.' Then Dixel realised. 'Oh, you *do* care. You want to get back into your old social circle.'

'I didn't say that.'

'You didn't have to. You said everything but, which clearly means you do.'

'What kind of logic is that?'

'The truth hurts.'

'Whatever.'

. . .

Ethan didn't want to be part of the conversation anymore, so he got on his board and skated off down the street ahead of Dixel.

'Hey, wait up.' Dixel shouted, getting on her board.

Ethan thought about what Dixel had said, it was true that he missed his old skate friends, but he wasn't sure whether it was possible to connect with them again anyway. Bridges had been burned. He often imagined what might happen if he bumped into Ren. He was sure they'd hug it out and catch up for lost time, and things would all be good. He knew that once he'd manage to befriend one, it would open the door to the others, but that first step felt impossible.

'Left here,' Dixel shouted at Ethan. 'I've got to go past the depot and collect my case.'

He took a sharp left, ollieing off the pavement and back on again. Dixel lagged at the back but did well to keep up. She could handle the corners if they were big enough, but anything tight and she needed to jump off, save the board from rolling out into the road, get back on and push off again. Ethan looked back at her occasionally but now she was quite a way back.

'Slow down a bit!' she shouted.

Ahead was a long tarmac road and very little traffic, except for some parked cars and white vans unloading at the back of the shops. It was slightly downhill and easy to coast to the bottom. Dixel found her balance and gradually built up speed. In less than a minute she had caught up to Ethan, as he made no effort to push and his bearings and little wheels had pretty much hit Mach 10 for their size.

'Ha-ha, I've caught up now!' she said once alongside him.

Then she started edging ahead, 'Hey, it's going too fast.'

'Don't jump off,' Ethan said. Too many times he had seen people freak out at speed and come off worse than if they'd stayed on. 'Just go with it and you'll be fine.'

Her board rolled forward, quiet, unassuming, and craving to go faster.

'What do I do? Should I jump off?'

Ethan realised there was no-way he could catch up with her, 'No. Stay on it. Crouch down and hold the sides of the board if you need to, but just go with it. You'll be alright. There's no traffic.'

It seemed as if her board was doubling in speed compared to Ethan's and eventually all he could do was shout, 'I'll meet you at the bottom,' but she was busy screaming.

At one point the board started to wobble and he thought she'd lose control, but a couple of seconds later, it straightened out again. He could see her reaching the bottom of the hill and knew she'd made it through the worst. As long as she didn't do anything stupid she'd be fine. He glanced back up the hill to check if the road was still clear then cruised down to the bottom.

Dixel was already off her board pacing around with a big grin. 'Oh my god,' she said. 'That was mental. Did you see how fast I was going?' She looked back up the hill surprised at the distance covered. 'I can now see why you skate. Is it always like this?'

'Look at you; Queen of the slight gradient,' Ethan said.

'I don't ever want to get used to that.' Dixel held out her hands. 'Look they're shaking.'

'It's a free fix you didn't need to smoke.'

After that, Dixel couldn't shut up about the ride of her life and Ethan would rather not be chasing a delivery distribution centre unless there was, a) something there to skate, or b) something better than skating, like a bikini contest. He'd already been to the depot once and knew neither was available. Besides the detour to the depot was a fruitless waste of time; it had closed for the day despite the sign saying they'd be open until 4pm. A driver could be seen through the glass and though Dixel caught his eye to open up, he didn't come to the door, he just flashed his watch, shrugged, and returned to moving pallets of boxes around on sack trucks. Dixel got on the phone and spoke with the head office. After giving them the tracking ID, she hung up.

'I can't believe it!' she said. 'They've sent it back to the Travelodge.'

'That's good right?'

'Maybe for you, but not for me. The more that thing moves the more I don't have it.' They both headed back to the Travelodge and she couldn't forgive their incompetence.

'They're only trying to get it back to you,' Ethan said.

'But they need to ask me first. What if I'd left and found another hotel? I'd then be chasing them to track it down again. It's crap that I continually have to put up with in my job.

'So, why are you doing it?' Ethan said.

17

THE SECOND CASE

At this point Dixel took a moment before answering. It was a good question; it was simple. Why? She'd asked him the same about his skating and yet she also didn't have a good answer.

'Chasing suitcases? Or the urban exploration?' Dixel thought some more. 'It's the most intense thing ever.'

'The same as skateboarding.'

'No, it isn't. You just goof around until you impress yourself or someone else. That's all it boils down to.'

'What you do is hardly intense.' Ethan tried to picture himself in the same situation. Surely setting up a camera and pressing the record button hardly matches the feeling of jumping down a set of stairs. 'How difficult could it be?'

'You'd be surprised,' Dixel said. 'Don't you

realise that you skate on the surface? Urban X is underground. It's not allowed. It's exploration of where people don't go for a good reason. You simply go where everyone goes. I'm bored by that. Give me somewhere that I can't see; somewhere no-one else has been, then, and only then, is my heart beating.'

'I think you're deluded. It only proves you know nothing about skateboarding. The clue is in the title: the places you go have been abandoned. The only thing to hold you back is a wire fence and a Keep Out sign. What's the challenge in that? Try doing the same with security guards chasing you all day.'

'But, that's because you're stupid. You're banging a drawing pin in with a lump hammer.'

'What?'

'There's no skill in your location. You just turn up and deal with whatever you're faced with. UX takes months of planning, sometimes years, the costs can be crazy, and the locations are all over the world.'

'Yeah, well, you wouldn't get me doing it. If I can't get there by boat, I'm not going.'

'Why not?'

Ethan paused. Whenever he'd mentioned his fear of flying in the past he'd always been mocked and knowing the little he knew about Dixel, it was clear she was going to give him a hard time about it as well. A wash of deja-vu came over him.

'I can't fly. I throw up.'

'Oh, you mentioned that earlier. Was the flight so bad?'

'No, that was just on the car journey to the airport. We stopped six times. It was bloody obvious I wasn't getting on that plane.'

'Have you ever spoken to anyone about it?'

'The doctor can't give me anything for it apart from some over the counter pills'

'No, I mean a head doctor.'

'Hey?'

'Forget it.'

At the Travelodge Dixel waited for the receptionist to finish rummaging in the back room for the case matching the description. She returned with a big secure box with padlocks on all sides.

'What's in there? Gold bars?' Ethan could see that the receptionist was equally as interested in the contents. She glanced at Ethan and raised her eyebrows due to the weight.

'Oh, you know. Just some girly things,' Dixel said. She thanked the receptionist, signed the paperwork and made her way over to the lift. 'Are you coming?'

'Not in there.' Ethan looked at Dixel in the elevator and just saw a free ticket to death via a budget maintenance contract and a cable being nibbled by rust. 'I don't do lifts for the same reason I don't fly.'

'Jesus Christ. Who damaged you as a baby? It's just one floor.'

He considered showing her that he could if he wanted to.

She held the door open.

'You're not taking no for an answer, are you?'

'No.'

Ethan took the stairs. The relief was immediate, and he let out a huge breath, then took several big breaths until he felt like he was calming down. It was 7 pm and he had three text messages from his girlfriend, Amy, and two missed calls. He didn't have time for a long call right now. He put the phone back in his pocket and got out of the stairwell onto the first floor.

'One flight of stairs,' Dixel said.

'Leave it out.'

Dixel rolled the heavy case across the hallway carpet and bumped it up against the wall as she took out her door pass. 'You want to see what real organisation looks like? Come in and I'll show you.'

She placed it on the bed and removed all the padlocks. She flipped the lid and lifted out a climbing harness and ropes. 'This,' she held up a metal device, 'is an Ascender, and this is a snap-gate, and this is a pulley, and three slings.'

'This is some kind of Fifty Shades stuff, right?' he said. 'I really don't know what I'm looking at.'

'You've not climbed, I take it?'

Ethan hadn't.

Dixel pulled out a foam layer and embedded within the slots was a number of…

'Electronics next.' Dixel took out a, 'GoPro Hero 5 and batteries, three of, again, and an Anker Powercore charger. It's not the best, but it works.'

Another foam layer was pulled out and placed on the bed, 'Next,' she said. 'The kitchen: 15 days of snacks, 11 days of freeze-dried meals, 6 days of cooked meals. This,' she placed her hand on a steel canister with a brown coating, 'a brand-new Jet Boil and purification tablets.'

The pile of equipment on the bed kept growing, as Dixel pulled another layer of foam out of the case.

'It looks like you're going into space for six months.'

'More like middle-earth for a few weeks.' She reached into the final slots of foam and pulled out a spotlight. These are a 1000 watt and I've got three of them.'

'You like threes.'

'It's a failsafe number. One failure, happens; two failures at the same time are incredibly unlikely; three failures at the same time? Statistically improbable and I can still get the job done.'

'Have you ever needed all that food?'

'Not yet.' Dixel placed the light head back down into the foam slot. 'I have enough batteries and power supply to keep everything running on full for 24 hours. I've never needed to do that either, but that's what I plan for. So, when I say that you just turn up and skate, this is what I mean. I have to plan for the world ending on every trip. Every location I visit is one where I might not be reached, or even found, for days.'

'I thought you filmed other photographers?'

'I do,' she said packing the gear back in again. 'But we often separate whilst looking for locations and there's a lot of time alone when things could go wrong.'

'Why can't you just phone someone?'

'How many nuclear bunkers do you know with phone reception or Wi-fi? It's not an option. Trust me.'

The equipment and the precision of how everything was packed in the case was impressive, but she didn't know his skateboard was made from the finest Canadian Maple money could buy. Seven layers of super-thin plies, set and glued with resin in a press for days before being cut to shape. The trucks weren't just lumps of metal, but specially designed using the finest alloy to give them the strength of steel with the weight of aluminium.

Then there were the wheels, special 84b 54mm SPF Bones.

'See these?' Ethan pointed to the bearings in his wheels, 'German precision engineered bearings tested at 1000s of revolutions per second.'

'I know,' she said without looking up. 'They use them in washing machines, don't they? Look, I really don't care much for what you choose to do, but if you're helping your brother out, well, then I guess I'm feeling a little guilty.'

'Why should you feel guilty? He's my brother.'

Dixel pointed to all the gear on the bed. 'All this means, we can still film the part. We just do it at night.'

'Really? But how? I mean, the noise, we'll be spotted immediately.'

'And? How long do we need?'

'Fifteen minutes of footage.'

'Edited?'

'Yep.'

'How good are you?'

Ethan shrugged. 'Pretty good.'

'I've got the filming part covered, you just need to do your part.'

Ethan still couldn't get his head around how they would be able to get in and out unnoticed with the minimum of disturbance. 'How do you mean you've got the filming covered? Those flood lights will draw attention like meat in a rat cage once you turn them on. Besides, should I bother?' Ethan said. 'I've missed the window to deliver the edit. They've probably fired me already.'

'Then don't do it for them. Do it for Heston. To prove you came all this way and did everything you could. From what you've told me, he's not expecting you to quit.'

'I suppose you're right. I don't care what Flint thinks.'

'There you go,' she said. 'And at least I get some filming done.'

'Because it's all about you?'

'No, because it can't always be about you.'

It was 9pm. 'Let's go out at midnight'

'No, that's too early,' she said. 'It should be just before daylight. Three or Four o'clock. We need to be sure there isn't anyone around.'

With the plan set and agreed, even if Ethan wasn't exactly sure of how the hell they'd pull it off, he had confidence in Dixel's planning, and that was enough for him. He went back to his room and called up room service only to be told, politely, there wasn't any.

There was a Subway next door.

'I don't believe they take orders over the phone,' the receptionist said.

18

THE BRONX

Ethan put on the TV and sent a text message to Heston.

Holed up for the night. Looking at sneaking a roll tomorrow. Sorry the footage didn't come through on time. I'll crawl up Flint's ass and beg forgiveness when I get back. How are you holding up?

He watched a documentary on Scientology for a few minutes before his phone pinged again.

Flint crucified me today. Don't worry, I shrugged it off. I think you can expect fireworks when you get back. I'm good. Physio was harsh and I'm aching like a mother here :/

· · ·

Ethan woke to Dixel banging on the door. The TV was still on and he was still in the same clothes.

'I've tried texting and calling you. You're not ready.'

'I'm good.'

'No, actually, you're not. Wash, you moron. I'll meet you downstairs, and hurry up, we've only got an hour until daylight.'

It was 3:25am when they got to the Braxton Estate and they tucked themselves into the bushes. The courtyard looked clear, so Dixel made her way over to the block, whilst Ethan went to a carpark across the street to warm up with a few skate tricks. She kept low and moved quickly, dropping her bags beside the block and setting up the floodlights. The first lamp was positioned about three meters to the left of the block and the second three metres to the right. A third lamp was placed head on and angled down as much as possible to stop the light from hitting the nearby windows. The sound of Ethan's board clacked and popped through the night air, but wasn't loud enough to twitch any curtains.

Dixel left the lamps and ran back to the hedge to grab the second case which contained her camera. As she was about to run back, a figure moved across one side of the building. She recognised the man's walk. It was Carl Needs.

'Shit,' she whispered.

Carl stopped at the block and took a look at her stuff on the floor. Her bag still had a combination lock on, which he couldn't open.

Dixel rang Ethan. 'Carl is back. I guess a lawyer got him released. Get over here.'

She watched Carl examine her lights, realising that he was calculating the resale value in his head.

'Don't you dare,' she muttered.

Just as Ethan arrived, Carl grabbed the first lamp and went for the second one. Dixel ran out from the bush, sprinted across the courtyard, and swiped the back of Carl's knee. He buckled briefly but regained his balance, then swung the lamp knocking her to the ground. Ethan arrived a split second later, and as he dived at Carl, he dodged out of the way and Ethan tumbled into the block.

Dixel got to her feet.

'Are you ok?'

'I'm fine,' she said, 'but that idiot needs sorting out.'

Ethan sprinted across the courtyard and burst through the entrance doors. He momentarily looked at the stairs and figured that Carl would have easily raced up all twenty floors. Ethan considered taking the lift, then looked back at the stairs. Neither appealed. One was a killer climb of infinite stairs and the other was a short fast ride in a death box. The only choice was how long did he want the suffering to be. *It's only one floor*, he remembered Dixel saying to him, *Think of it as just one floor*. Then as if someone had made the choice for him, the lift doors opened, a man was briefly startled to see Ethan pacing around, clearly agitated by the weight of his decision.

The man gave an awkward smile and side-stepped uneasily past him. After taking a few quick breaths, Ethan threw himself into the lift as the doors began to close and held onto the handrails in a corner. The doors slid shut, gently sealed them-selves together, and it took another five painfully long seconds before the overhead motor clunked and whirred into action. The cables tightened and Ethan felt his bodyweight press into the soles of his feet. His entire body tensed, leaving only the flabby, fleshy, uncontrollable parts to flex with the change in gravity. Tiny gears clicked together, and the lift frame scraped against the outer wall of the shaft. The speed slowly increased. He shut his eyes and tried to picture a walk on the beach to calm his breathing. He tried to concentrate on the sound of the waves, and the sand between his toes, warmth on his skin and that good sea breeze. He didn't want to open his eyes and be reminded of being shut in a creaking metal death vessel. He heard the waves crash, washing up against the lift and felt like it was slowly sinking into the sand. He couldn't get out and slapped his palms repeatedly on the small windows until they stung. No-one could hear him shouting for help on the beach. Sunbathers saw him and waved back. The lift began to sink deeper into the sand, the waves kept crashing harder and harder against the tiny windows. He smashed one with his elbow and tried to attract someone's attention. The waves kept crashing and flooding the container, until the lift tilted and fell onto its side.

Ethan's legs gave way and dropped him onto the cold and filthy lift floor.

The sea-salt spray stung his eyes. Dixel peered through the broken window and held up her phone to display zero-zero in red LEDs. *It's only one floor*, she said over and over. The number changed to zero one.

It's only one floor, he thought. *It's only one floor.*

A bulb in the ceiling behind a frosted plastic sheet—home to a dozen dead flies and a curious yellowing stain in one corner—blinked off and on once. It happened so quickly that he wasn't sure if it really happened. The thought of being plunged into darkness stopped his breath and he counted three heartbeats in his ears.

Don't. Please don't.

His breath was staccato short and his skin pricked with heat. His neck hairs felt a thin line of cool sweat where fabric met flesh. He tried to focus on the beach again, and for a moment, it worked, until, with a small and barely audible pop, the tiny filament in the bulb broke and the lift went black. He shouted into the air so hard his throat hurt, whilst the dry and rusty winches screeched. In the darkness of the small cubical the small LED floor numbers blinked softly. Floor six meant there were fourteen more to go, and there was nothing he could do about it. The lift rattled and clunked its way up the shaft, knocking itself into the internal frame, as if some giant decided to prod the cage of a pet with a stick just to see what it would do.

'Stop screwing with me!' Ethan shouted into the void.

He watched the floor indicator click over from eleven to twelve. Eight more floors. *Come on, Jesus Christ, come on.* He took some more deep breaths and fought against a growing urge to punch the button for floor fourteen which would release him from the box. He gave up trying to calm himself with thoughts of the beach, instead he focused on Carl's face in Flat 882 that he wanted to slam into the wall. He sat up and watched the floor numbers. Seventeen clicked over to eighteen. Just a couple more to go.

Why the hell did Carl have to live this high up? Why didn't Dixel go get her lights herself?

Floor eighteen clicked over to nineteen and the lift began to slow, then it stopped. One floor short.

That would do. He could run the rest of the way, just one floor, he could do it. The lift door didn't open and a crack of light didn't pierce through the wall.

Had the lift broken? Maybe someone was getting on?

Nothing happened.

'Hello?!' He pounded on the door with his nose pressed into the join, hoping a sound would leak through. 'Can anyone hear me?'

19

FLAT 882

Trapped on the nineteenth floor, he pounded his
fists against the doors again and again. He remembered the light on his phone and used it to illumi-
nate the control panel and locate the alarm button.
With his thumb jamming into it multiple times, he
feared that too had stopped working, so he held it
in, until eventually the doors slid open. Ethan fell
out into the cool air, and after a moment of trying
to calm down, he realised he was angry that Carl
had forced him into this situation. He got up and
burst through the doors to the stairwell and ran up
the last of the steps two at a time until he reached
floor twenty. At Carl's flat, he stood back, aimed at
the door lock and kicked. It broke away from the
weak wooden frame. At the end of the hallway, Carl
was on his phone, and before he could move Ethan
slammed into him. Carl never stood a chance

against Ethan's intentions. Despite very little struggling whilst he twisted Carl's wrist behind him, Ethan enjoyed accidentally knocking his knee into Carl's head. Once Carl was complying and in pain, Ethan attempted the same leg lock Dixel used. After a couple of attempts he had it. Carl was pinned with a finger. That wasn't enough, he needed to make sure Carl couldn't leave whilst they finished their filming. A leather belt on a small table was a perfect fit around Carl's knees. After pulling it tight there was no-way he could move. Next, he pulled out a long Timberland boot lace and used it to tie Carl's hands together; he tried to resist until Ethan pushed on the leg lock and triggered so much pain in Carl's knee joint that he thrust his hands forward, almost begging to be tied.

'Are you in too much pain?' Ethan said after completing the knot.

Carl nodded through clenched teeth.

'Good. Now stay there whilst I get my job done, and if you're lucky I'll call the Police to come and free you later.'

Dixel stepped in through the doorway and placed her cases down. 'What the hell happened here? What did I miss?'

'What do you think of my handiwork?' Ethan said with a smile. 'Pretty good, huh?'

'We've got a problem: the floodlights are too powerful. I tested one lamp and even the ambient light lit up the first four floors... of three tower blocks. It's too much. We'll be lucky to get two minutes before someone shows up again. We need something else.'

'Carl?' Ethan said walking towards the back room where he stashed his gear. 'Have you been naughty and collected anything else in here?' After turning on the light, he saw the room as packed with stolen goods again as if it hadn't been cleared out yesterday. 'Jesus, Dixel. Look at this.'

'Wow, you're a fast mover.'

Together they looked over all the electronic gadgets, boxes, and shelving, pulling out devices, trying to figure out if any of them would be any good. They found nothing more powerful than LCD screens and weak desk lamps.

'There's nothing here. It's useless,' Dixel said.

Ethan picked out a metal headset and flipped it over in his hands and put it on. 'There must be something here. Are you sure we can't use your lamps? What if we make a shield for them?'

Dixel just looked at him as if confused.

'You know,' Ethan continued, 'maybe we could place some card over the bulbs and block out the light.'

Dixel walked a little closer to Ethan with a confused look on her face.

'Uh, personal space, please,' he said leaning back slightly. 'What's the matter with you?'

Dixel squinted at the thing on his head, 'What the hell is that?' She reached up and pulled the headset off of him and held it closer. 'I think these are night vision goggles.'

'So?'

'Can you ride in the dark with them?'

'Maybe, but why?'

'We're not going to need any light. My camera has a thermal imaging mode.'

'Really?'

'Yes. It's not just some dumb old Sony.'

Dixel walked out into the light of the hallway with the goggles.

'Wait,' Ethan said. 'Why do you have a thermal…? Oh, forget it.'

Taking the stairs back down was much easier than Ethan expected, whether he just had no energy left to fight it, or maybe the stairs were a breeze compared to being shut in the lift, he wasn't sure. His phone torch lit the way, concentrating on each step, yet he didn't even seem to notice the levels in-between. He was replaying the action of the day: his scrap with Carl, and Dixel's camera idea was perfect. They'd release the footage online and Flint would regret dropping him. She needed to suffer his Slings and Arrows for a change.

By the time he got down to the courtyard, Dixel

had set everything up again. The lamps were in position and her camera had been swapped for what resembled a handheld police radar gun.

'I rarely get chance to shoot in darkness,' she said switching on the power, 'so this will be a good test. Here, put the headset back on.'

Ethan pulled the nylon strap down over his chin and positioned the lenses over his eyes. Dixel flicked the switch on the side and the darkness blinked into vague green shapes.

'Can you see anything?'

'I can see something, but not very well.'

Dixel guided his fumbling fingers onto the adjustment ring until all the edges became crisp; it was as if all the surfaces had been coated with a toxic paint. The hardest thing to see was Dixel's face.

'Why can't I see you?'

'Maybe it can't deal with smooth contours.'

Ethan examined his open hands under the new light and closed his fingers into a fist.

'Start riding,' she said. 'You need to get used to that lump on your head.'

He jumped on his board and explored his new animated world, ollieing a couple of times, and then manual-rolling the block. The clattering of the wheels in the cracks echoed across the tower blocks. People would certainly hear him, however, without working streetlights in the courtyard, they wouldn't see a thing. After trying a couple of flips his confidence grew. 'I think I've got a handle on it,' he said. 'Are you good to go?'

'You bet.' Dixel turned on the camera and Ethan lit up in a yellow and orange glow of heat. She adjusted the resolution until his shape formed perfectly. 'It looks like you're hovering, I can only see a faint edge of the board and it looks trippy.'

Ethan hit the block with a frontside lip-slide, locking it in behind the front-truck, and sliding it to the end.

'How's it looking?'

'Just keep riding and let me worry about that.'

The second line consisted of a perfect kickflip backside 50-50.

'Hey, your wheels must be warming up, I can see little lines appearing on the concrete behind you.'

Ethan rolled back around and ollied up frontside 180 into a fakie nose-grind and popped a shove-it out. The block felt good and the headset wasn't bothering him at all. The more tricks he did the easier it got.

'Keep the noise down,' someone shouted down from one of the flats, just as Ethan did a frontside tail-slide.

From across the courtyard a police car slowed to a stop and the officer wound down the window. Despite the clattering sound of wood on concrete coming from the flats the officer remained in his car and listened.

Ethan ollied up into a nose-wheelie and slid the board across into a frontside nose-blunt. His wheels squeaked against the dry granite surface and caused another shout from one of the flats. Only then did the officer reluctantly grab his torch and leave his vehicle.

'How much more?' Dixel said.

'A few more lines should do it.'

Ethan circled around to take another run at the block, but slowed up as he saw the torch light cut across the courtyard and the silhouette of a man walking towards them. It wasn't until he got close and dipped the light that they realised it was the same officer who took Carl away yesterday.

'What are you doing here?' the officer said.

'Uh, nothing much,' Dixel said. 'We're just filming that's all.'

'You're making a lot of noise and disturbing the residents, I hear.'

'No, we're not, and we're almost done.' Ethan took off the headset. 'We're not doing any harm, seriously.'

'I think otherwise,' the officer said.

'Hey, what happened to Carl?' Ethan said trying to distract him. 'Yesterday we thought we weren't going to see him for a while, but I see he's back already.'

The officer flicked his torch over to Dixel, then back again at Ethan, and seemed to reconsider their immediate threat on the locals. 'Hmm,' he said bringing the torch light to a spot on the ground. 'We hoped to put him away for a while, but there wasn't enough evidence. We had to let him go, but he's on a curfew, so he's no real threat to anyone.'

'What do you mean by a curfew?' Dixel asked. 'Like, he can't go a certain distance from his home?'

'No.' The officer gave a little chuckle. 'This curfew means he can't even step out of his house. Total shut down.'

'Uh,' Ethan said looking at Dixel. They both thought the same thing. 'What if he did?'

'Then we'd have reason to arrest him immediately and he'd be held until trial for breach of a court order.'

Ethan smiled.

'What is it?' the officer said.

'He's been out tonight. We both had a run in with him again.'

'Perfect,' the officer said. 'And you're happy to make a statement to support that?'

'Sure,' Dixel said. 'We both are.'

'But,' Ethan interrupted, 'I don't think you're going to need us. We chased him back up to his flat and found the room was full of stolen gear again.'

'He's up there now,' Dixel said. 'Hog-tied.'

'Really?' The officer pulled out his radio. 'And you phoned the police immediately, right?'

'Uh,' Ethan hesitated. 'We just wanted to get this done first.'

'Right. Well please stay here while I go check it out.' The officer walked away quickly towards the tower block and radioed for assistance. As soon as he was inside the doors, Ethan knew it was now or never to finish what they started.

'Let's do it,' he said.

20

GOING THERMAL

Ethan put the headset back on and attacked the block one more time. Frontside crook, backside 5-0 to switch crook, nose-slide to fakie nose-grind, and backside 50-50 to nollie-flip out. Within a few runs Dixel had captured enough footage to meet the 10-trick minimum Ethan needed. Lights had started to go on in people's homes. It was approaching 4am, and though he had some comfort in the Police officer being nearby, they knew that they needed to get out of there before someone came out and made them move.

'Are we done?' Dixel said.

Ethan nodded, 'Time to go.'

Dixel went back to her case and began putting away the camera. Silence fell in the darkness again, and Ethan looked up at the top floor and tried to picture the delight of the officer's face upon seeing Carl and enough new stolen goods to put him away for a while. Suddenly Ethan felt like something was nearby. It was too quiet. He looked into the blackness and felt as if someone was very close to them.

'Do you feel that?' he said but she didn't hear him. Ethan walked a few paces forward towards the edge of the courtyard, he put his hand on the low fencing and listened. There was a light amber, a tapping, a slight jangle of chain. *What is that?* He thought. A snarling pit-bull leapt out over the fencing and locked onto his arm. He fell back and landed on the floor, just as two other dogs leapt over the fence and joined the first. All three had their jaws locked on his arms and leg. They snarled and whipped their bodies around as he rolled about but no matter what he tried, nothing would shake their ferocious grip. He rolled over and over flipping the dogs around attempting to crush them with his weight. Dixel's efforts to pull the dogs away by their hind legs failed. Ethan got on top of one of the animals and pushed his free knee into the neck of a dog on his arm. He increased the pressure as much as he could until its eyes bulged, and although the dog held tight the pressure on its head was obvious. Its eyes looked like they were about to pop out yet despite all the whimpering its jaw remained tight. A pair of hands reached down onto Ethan's leg and tried to pull him away.

'Don't. Don't. It's working,' he said believing it to be Dixel.

But it wasn't, the dog owner pushed Ethan over, releasing the pressure, called the dog's name out, then shouted a command to *release*. All the dogs instantly let go of him.

As quick as they arrived they were gone. Ethan only saw the trainers and tracksuit bottoms of the owner run off towards the flats.

'Are you okay?' Dixel said.

Ethan sat up and used the light of her phone to inspect the damage. The dogs had drawn blood on both arms and his leg. Two clean puncture wounds on each forearm and a small patch of blood seeping through onto his jeans.

'Yeah, it's just a scratch.'

'You're going to need a Doctor.'

'No, I'll be okay. I've had my shots.'

'Don't be stupid. You've just been mauled and need to get those wounds...' Dixel stopped herself, as it was clear Ethan wasn't listening. 'Ok, whatever. You'll be fine. You okay to walk?'

Dixel held out her hand and helped him up. After a little pacing around he was able to move enough to leave. She packed the last of her gear in the case, put Ethan's headset in her bag and zipped it closed. Whilst walking back across the courtyard, they saw another police car arriving and decided to stay out of the way in case of further questioning.

The officer didn't see them in the dark and ran towards the doors of the flats. They both walked out to the main road and managed to catch a bus back to the Travelodge.

Ethan bought a small first aid kit out of the vending machine and followed Dixel up the single flight of stairs to his room.

'You sure you don't need any help?'

'Well, uh, you could…'

'I mean from a Doctor, not me.'

'Oh right. No, I'm good. I'll just take a bath. You get some sleep.'

'Are you kidding?' she laughed and walked off towards her room. 'You think this footage is going to edit itself?'

Ethan woke from the buzz of a call from reception.

'Mr Wares, I need to make you aware that your leaving time is 11am. If you plan on staying longer, you will need to book for another night. Would you like me to make that arrangement now?'

'What time is it?'

'It's midday. We have cleaners waiting to get into your room.'

Ethan tried to sit up and noticed his arm and leg were stuck to the sheets by congealed blood.

'Can you give me a little more time? I've over-slept. My alarm didn't go off.'

'We can give you until 1pm, but we will need to charge another £20.'

A whole day was £40 and the receptionist insisted that was the correct rate. Ethan thought for a moment. 'Can you tell me if Ms Manning in room 203 has left?'

'Yes. She left at 11.'

Ethan sat for a moment wondering why she didn't wake him. She knew his room number, but she hadn't knocked or got reception to phone him.

He agreed to extend his stay and once the arrangement had been made, the receptionist told him the bill would be made up for him to collect at the desk.

'Wait. Are you still there?' Ethan said almost hanging up the call. 'Did Ms Manning leave a message for me?'

'There's nothing on the system, Mr Wares.'

'Thanks.' He hung up the phone and laid back on the pillow, and thought about why she'd left in such a hurry. It would have been nice to see the video edit. Maybe she hadn't been able to complete it, which would explain her leaving without saying goodbye.

On the way to the train station Heston called.

'What was that all about?'

'What are you on about? What was what?'

'You've not seen the edit? Just get to a TV screen as the repeat is running again in a few minutes.'

'What's wrong?' Ethan saw a TV shop across the road and dodged through the traffic to get a closer look at what channels were playing. 'Was the edit bad?'

'No. The edit was great. Event Flint loves it, I mean, considering it wasn't what she was expecting and she still plans to fire you.'

Ethan went inside the shop and looked at the TVs on the wall. There was a young man behind the counter in a black shirt staring into his phone.

'Can I help you, sir?'

Ethan saw the man—John, Sales Executive— look him up and down. A look Ethan was used to.

'Can you do me a favour I just need to look at this TV.' He pointed towards a large flat screen beside the desk. 'Can you put it on Channel 27?'

'I'm sorry sir, but if you're interested in buying, I can help you, but…'

'Yes, of course, I'm interested in buying.' Ethan picked up the remote at the base of the TV. 'Does this thing work?' He called up the channel on the screen and watched the tail end of an advert, then he saw the familiar N27 logo roll across the bottom of the screen.

'It's coming up now,' he said to Heston.

The screen faded to black and large letters

appeared across the centre of the screen. 'Coming soon to N27. Urban Explorer. Dixel Manning takes you to some of the most incredible locations ever.' A series of still shots of building interiors and double-speed footage of exterior panoramas strobed on the screen.

'What the?' Ethan said. 'I didn't know about this. Is there any skating at all?'

'None. Keep watching.'

Some incredible HDR panoramas glided across the screen then some time-lapse footage of a sun rise from inside an abandoned building with a huge ornate staircase came into view, a school room, a military bunker, and what appeared to be a medical facility.

'The talk on-line is good too. But people believe your show is being replaced.'

'I'm on my way back now.' Ethan checked the time. 'It'll take a couple of hours. Will everyone still be there?'

'Don't bother. Just come in tomorrow. Flint's booked the conference room for a meeting so we'll see you after that.'

Ethan told Heston he'd see him there and hung up the phone. The salesman tried to hand Ethan a brochure about their finance packages, but he was already walking out of the building. *How could she do that to me?* He thought. He got straight on the phone to Dixel and called her.

A man's voice said hello.

'Dixel?'

'No, sorry. I think you've got the wrong number, mate.'

Ethan checked the number again, saw it was correct, and then threw his phone into the wall beside him.

21

THE SWITCH

Ethan pushed open the door to the Planet office to find Flint waiting for him. Dixel glanced up, looked back at Flint, and then over to Heston. She was clearly uncomfortable and Ethan enjoyed watching her fidget as he took a seat.

'Thank you for coming in,' Flint said.

Flint's politeness was all for Dixel. In the five years of meetings, she'd never once thanked him for anything, even Heston felt unnerved by her tone.

'I must say,' Flint continued, 'that you've put us, the team, the board, in quite a situation. No doubt Heston has informed you that the edit was not what we expected. Yet, from what I'm told, if it wasn't for Ms Manning, we wouldn't have received anything at all. So, for that we should be grateful.' Flint smiled at Dixel. Ethan wanted to explode, but bit his tongue.

Flint looked at a report sheet. 'It appears, judging by the viewing figures, that Ms Manning's footage proved very popular. However, that doesn't change the fact that you, Ethan, were under contract to deliver and failed.'

Flint pulled across an envelope and slid it across the desk to Ethan.

He picked it up.

'Go ahead,' Flint said. 'It's yours.'

The envelope was thin and flimsy in his hands, and contained only a single sheet of paper which headlined the end of his contract.

'You're firing me?' Ethan's heart sank and it felt like the day everyone else fired him. It wasn't his fault, he worked his ass off, and this was the thanks they gave him.

'Yes. Well, technically you fired yourself; count this as confirmation.'

Ethan couldn't believe what was happening. After what he and Dixel had been through to capture the edit at the Braxton Estate, this was how they'd repay him.

'This,' Flint said holding up a piece of headed notepaper which he couldn't quite read. 'Is your new contract. If you agree to it of course.'

'You're hiring me, again?'

'It's a technicality. Think of it as rewriting your position here. This new contract, voids every privilege you had previously, yet it offers a position to work with Ms Manning on a new show, based on a number of KPIs…'

KPIs sounded like something fried in a bucket.

'Key Performance Indicators,' Flint said. 'It's a metric we'll use to decide if you're delivering.'

'Don't tell me, Bennett devised this?' Ethan knew that anything involving a spreadsheet would have been penned by accounts.

'Yes. It's now standard across the network. But these are merely details. You just need to work with Ms Manning and deliver, as before. She's your permanent camera operator and editor.'

'Wait, what?' Dixel said. 'I thought we agreed that I'd be working alone.'

'We're still looking into that option for you. Until then, well, you've got to be doing something around here. Ms Manning will be finding locations, filming and editing remotely. Considerably reducing the man hours required at this end.'

'Um,' Heston interrupted. 'But I do that.'

'Did,' Flint said. 'We're looking into your role, and feel a reorganisation may be required.'

Flint closed up her file and put her pen in her top pocket. 'This is good, people.' She stood and pushed her chair back under the table. 'I'm feeling unusually positive about the new format. Now, I have to be at another meeting, I'm sure you're all keen to discuss the new working arrangements?

Unless of course, Ethan, you're not keen to take the job?'

Everyone looked at him, and in the moment, he felt as if he had been royally shafted. Nothing from Flint was ever in his favour. What was his alternative?

'I guess,' Ethan said.

'Good.' Flint placed the new contract down in front of him. 'Sign on the dotted line and let's get to work.'

Once the contract had been signed Flint whipped the paper out from under his pen before it had even left the page.

Heston stood up and walked to the door before Flint could leave.

'I, uh,' he said quietly. 'I would like to have a chat with you as soon as possible about the new position. I'm sure I can be valuable in some other capacity.'

'Well, that remains to be seen. As I said, everything is under review and we'll have an outline for you as soon as we can.'

With that Flint left the three of them together.

'What a bitch,' Dixel said.

'The same could be said about you,' Ethan said.

'Screw you. Didn't you get my messages? I tried to warn you?'

'What messages?'

'I texted you.'

Heston chuckled. 'Let's see it.'

Ethan pulled the phone out of his pocket and showed the smashed screen. 'Sorry, I didn't get them. Were they important?'

'Yes,' she said. 'Because they would have stopped you asking lots of stupid questions.'

Heston sat back down in the chair next to Ethan. 'Jesus,' Heston said. 'You heard her. I'm being fired.'

'She didn't say that,' Ethan said.

'She didn't have to.'

'She did,' Dixel said.

'Shut up,' Ethan said. 'You're not helping.'

'Well, it's fine for you,' Dixel said. 'You're the only one who got what they wanted here.'

'You got a job too. And what was all that bull-shit about our edit?'

'And here come those stupid questions I mentioned earlier. If you hadn't destroyed your phone, you would have known not to sign the contract. I put your skating edit online on my own account and it went ballistic. Everyone is talking about it and enquiries are arriving from loads of companies. You could probably cut a deal with someone better than this place.'

Ethan grabbed Heston's phone and checked his feed. She was right, page after page of notifications congratulating him. He scrolled for what seemed like forever.

'Told you,' Dixel said.

Ethan, Dixel and Heston gathered outside the N27 office. Heston's car was waiting, and he threw his crutches in on the back seat and climbed, slowly, into the passenger side.

'You need a lift?' Heston asked.

He looked up at the blue sky and then back at Heston.

'Hey, I was just offering; if I didn't, you'd only whine at me. Where are you heading?'

'To the park, probably. Or somewhere along the way.'

'Are you pissed at the outcome?'

Ethan was. Not only had his opportunity to leave N27 disappeared, but he was stuck with Dixel. 'Are you going to be okay?' he asked.

'I don't know.' Heston squeezed the steering wheel until his knuckles whitened. 'I knew Flint wanted you out, but I never imagined she'd flip it around like that.' Then Heston chuckled briefly to himself. 'And to think of the number of times I covered for you.'

'I didn't ask for this,' Ethan said. 'I thought I was out. I might be employed but I'm trapped. They've got me by the balls, again. You'll be fine. Look at me. You think that I've got any longevity in this company? It's only a matter of time and I'll be dropped, again. Whilst you, you've got brains. People always buy brains.'

'Stop with the damn compliments. I don't want this. I want to be doing what you do.'

'But you're making good progress with the physio, right?'

'Don't talk to me about progress. They can't tell me when I'll be able to drop the crutches.' Heston told his driver to leave and the car reversed out of the parking spot.

'I'm sorry about the edit switch,' Dixel said. 'But, look at it from my perspective: Flint was firing you anyway and I'm trying to get my foot in the door. You might feel that I stabbed you in the back, but geez, you've got views into the six figures on YouTube, and you've still got a job that pays you to skate.'

Ethan knew she was right, but didn't want to give her the satisfaction. 'So, what happens now?'

'I wait. We wait. Until Flint gets my contract sorted I'm not doing a thing.'

'You haven't signed one already?'

'No, my agent is looking over it.'

'You have an agent?'

'Like, duh,' she said. 'There's no way I'd read all that small print and understand it, besides, my man is going to negotiate for more.'

Ethan suddenly felt a little stupid for signing.

'He's going to rip a big cut for himself, though, right?'

'Not if he can't raise the price. If he gets me anything over the offer, he gets ten percent.'

'Things have sure moved on from when I first started. Agents? Next you'll have a personal assistant.'

Dixel held her eye contact with Ethan.

'You do?'

'Not exactly, but a virtual assistant, yeah. They handle my calls and emails. What? This isn't the dark ages. Have you not used the Internet in the last five years?'

'Shit, you're barely out of Uni.'

'Don't patronise me,' she said. 'You're barely out of rehab. I'm doing things right from day one. Didn't your parents teach you anything?'

Dixel stopped talking and let the edge subside a little. Ethan couldn't believe that he was being trumped so smoothly.

'Hey, thanks for the board though,' she said kicking it into her hand. 'I love it. But, honestly, does it make me look like a dork?'

'A bit, I'd say. But not completely.'

'How do I un-dork myself?'

'Skate every day and get a shorter board.'

'Ok, thanks for the tip.'

Ethan slipped his bag over his shoulders and then saw Dennis the security guard up ahead of him. 'You're still here?' Ethan said. 'Wow, I'm amazed.'

'Yep. They couldn't get rid of me. Fresh blood and a good work ethic never fails, unlike El Gato,' he said.

Ethan hit the brakes, 'He's gone?'

'He got wind that N27 changes were coming and couldn't bear the thought of being booted. So, he quit.'

'What's he doing now?'

'He's starting up his own private security firm.'

'Great. Just what the world needs.'

'Now get out of here before I zap you again.'

Dennis smiled and Ethan fist bumped him.

'Another time.'

Dennis pulled out his taser and cracked a spark, 'Hopefully not.'

BOOK 2: ABANDONED SAMPLE

1

MUSGRAVE PARK

It was eleven o'clock when Ethan Wares rolled into Musgrave skate park; a small and heavily graffitied local facility built fifteen years ago, full of precast blocks, banks and quarters, lazily cemented together. Eleven was the hour of beginners. Saturdays were the preference of parents, tourists, and the keen kids getting some practice in before the headcount reached double digits. As Ethan rolled casually around, he felt uncomfortable. Eleven was their hour, their time, not his. A few light tricks would get the legs going, a little ollie over the hip, a manual roll, and a shove-it. Other kids would have stumbled, wobbled, or fallen by now. Other kids would have approached the rail with trepidation, desperately ambitious with their focus, but wobbling with uncertainty as the slide drifted or stuck. Ethan's 50-50, however, did not. It landed with a solid confident clank, scraped consistently to the end, and landed with his dry spinning bearings whispering shhhhhhhhhhhh. He noticed a few lads had stopped skating. It was pointless holding back. They all knew he was there, they all knew he could ride, so there was no point pretending. He popped a frontside shove-it over the hip and ollied over the small spine. The kids sat down. Ethan moved closer to some that were still standing and they moved away. He stuck his nose into his shirt and sniffed his armpits.

Musgrave Park was where he and Ricard Flint chose to meet. Ethan called the time, as it had to be early enough to avoid his old crew. It'd been a few months of careful planning to avoid as many people as possible and it was proving to be easier than he'd hoped.

The top bank had a huge platform which fed into a handrail and hardly anyone bothered with. Most people avoided it and headed straight for the little fun box, but Ethan loved it. He rode down off the bank, floated lazily over the box and turned into a smith grind on the transition.

The coping was drier than he anticipated and it locked up, forcing him to run out and nearly hit a kid chasing after his stray board.

'I'm sorry,' said the kid. Once he'd grabbed it he walked back and said how much he enjoyed the show last week. 'I couldn't watch it properly because my sister kept grabbing the iPad.' The kid kept looking away like he wasn't supposed to be talking to a pro. He said he loved the shows and had watched the whole back catalogue as soon as he discovered it. During a moment where the boy felt at a loss for words, Ethan helped him out.

'You want a signature?'

The kid beamed with joy—he was only young —and Ethan took a sharpie from his pocket and signed his board.

'Can you write it to Matt?' The kid thanked him and grinned all the way back to his mates, stoked. Ethan was stoked too.

It took another twenty-minutes of grinds on the driveway box and little ollies out of the banks until Ricard's silver Honda pulled into the carpark. He popped the boot open, grabbed his board, and breezed into the park looking like a TV advert: light grey tracksuit bottoms, a loose-fitting navy blue shirt, and a beanie. It would have made sense if he was sponsored by GAP, but he actually bought that stuff himself. He might as well have ram-raided Oxfam covered in superglue.

'Hey, E,' Ricard said. 'I haven't been here for a while. Jesus, it's bad.'

'I have no problems.'

'I've seen you blast it,' Ricard said and handed Ethan a plastic A4 file.

Ricard skated off around the park with his

sloppy and lazy style; as if his trucks needed a couple of extra turns. There might as well have been cones on the flat the way he snaked around trying to decide which direction to go. Ethan set the file down on the driveway, opened it, and read the first page: Ubley Psychiatric Hospital.

'Fuck,' Ethan said as Ricard rolled up behind him.

'What's the matter?'

'It's the old Hospital; the worst location.'

'But, I asked you and you said yes.'

His shitty phone connection had let him down again. 'No,' Ethan stressed, 'anything other than the Hospital. We gave you five other locations. Why not any of those?'

'Sorry, I was trying to help you out.' Ricard held up his hands as if he was being mugged.

Ethan muttered quietly to himself and flipped quickly through a few of the pages. Nothing was read. He was thinking about what to do next.

Ricard left it a moment, but his head itched with a thought, 'If you didn't want to skate there, why submit it?'

What were the chances of the location he didn't want coming up? One-in-six it seemed, Ethan couldn't believe it. Whilst whittling down the potentials this was the one Dixel favoured. Sure there was some mystery behind the building since it had been shut down thirty-years earlier, but as a place to skate, it was a wreck compared to the other choices. The reality of pulling off a great edit in a crappy spot slowly dawned on him.

'So, that's it? We can't switch?'

It was futile and pointless asking. 'Yeah, yeah, I know. It's a waste of time.'

'Look,' Ricard said. 'I know you don't get on with my Aunt, but what I don't get is…' Ricard considered his words for a moment, 'Why don't you just quit?'

Ricard's Aunt, and director of entertainment, Celina Flint was fresh mud in the cracks of Ethan's shoes. He'd was fed up of explaining it. Ricard obviously hadn't got the email. His contract came with benefits he needed; break it and he'd lose them: the wage, his bonus would also go, as well as his company shares. And, crucially, there was the non-compete clause that prevented him from having a similar job for any other company for years. They had him by the balls. Leaving was easy; it was the living he had trouble with.

'Look you must be able to do something,' Ethan said. 'Can't you tell her this location is a rating-killer?'

Ricard just shrugged. He had a vested interest in Ethan failing anyway.

A kid rolled up to them and asked Ethan for a signature. He signed the bottom of the board and handed it back to him. The kid didn't go away.

'What's that?' the kid asked, and then after real-ising it was a location, asked, 'Where is it? Can I see?'

Ethan showed him the label on the folder.

The kids' face lit up, 'When are you going? Can we come and watch? I heard people had died and they left the bodies there.'

It was sad to tell the kid, no, no, and no, to all his questions, but they couldn't risk letting anyone near the building when filming. It was all too easy these days for footage to leak online.

'Too risky,' Ricard said. 'Total secrecy, remem-ber. If anyone finds out, it'll be cancelled.'

'I won't tell anyone,' the kid said turning back to his mates and shouting, 'He's going to the Psycho home!'

OTHER TITLES

Read the rest of the Ethan Wares Skateboard
series now:

Book 2: Abandoned
Book 3: Pool Staker
Book 4: Punch Drunk
Book 5: Nutbar DIY

AUTHOR'S NOTE

If you liked this story and would be interested in reading more, you can join my mailing list at https://skatefiction.co.uk and become one of my beta readers who get early access to new stories, give feedback, and receive reader copies in advance.

If you loved the book, please leave a positive review wherever you purchased it as this is the main way good books spread and help people discover me.

Thanks - Mark

ABOUT THE AUTHOR

Mark Mapstone is a UK skateboarder, writer, and author of the Ethan Wares Skateboard Series books.

After discovering there were no fiction books written for skateboarders with realistic skateboarding in them, and being qualified with a degree in creative writing from the prestigious Bath Spa University, Mark decided he was perfectly positioned to cater this audience.

In-between road-trips, an infinite Instagram feed of videos to watch, and discovering bruises on himself which he has no-idea how they got there, Mark uses his knowledge of the current skateboarding world to create exciting and authentic stories which every skateboarder goes through daily.

Follow Mark on Instagram: @7plywood.